Finding Parker

A Love story

Scott Hildreth

This book is a work of fiction. Names, characters, places, and incidents are the product of the author's imagination or are used fictitiously. Any resemblances to actual events, locales, or persons living or dead, are coincidental.

Copyright © 2014 by Scott Hildreth

All rights reserved. In accordance with the U.S. Copyright Act of 1976, the scanning, uploading, and electronic sharing of any part of this book without the permission of the author or publisher constitute unlawful piracy and theft of the author's intellectual property. If you would like to use the material from the book (other than for review purposes), prior written permission must be obtained by contacting the author at designconceptswichita@gmail.com. Thank you for your support of the author's rights.

Published by
Eralde Publishing

Cover Design Copyright © Creative Book Concepts
Text Copyright © Scott Hildreth
Formatting by Polgarus Studio

ISBN 13: 978-0-6923-1424-1
All Rights Reserved

DEDICATION

With red swollen eyes, and a heart filled with warmth,
I dedicate this book to my father.
Pop, this one is for you.

PROLOGUE

"In your professional opinion?" I looked out the window and waited for him to respond.

"My opinion would be just that, an opinion. As far as medical facts go, it's hard to…" the doctor began to explain.

"I did not ask for medical facts. I requested an opinion. Entertain me," my voice was remarkably calm considering the response I expected to receive.

"I've never been one to give opinions, but if you insist," the phone went silent as he paused for a moment.

The sound of breathing confirmed his presence on the phone. I gazed through the glass and into the courtyard as I waited for a response he was obviously uncomfortable providing. As I scanned the grounds for landscaping imperfections, he began to speak.

"It's difficult to say with any degree of certainty, but my *opinion* would be as follows," he took a shallow breath.

"Foregoing any treatment, I suspect between six months and a year. Treatment, as I have continued to express, could be one hundred percent successful. We have seen great successes with chemotherapy and radiation, especially at this stage. You are well aware of my professional recommendation, and I reserve hope you'll change your mind," he paused, hoping for a favorable response.

"Thanks, Doc. Six months it is. I'll make arrangements holding onto the hope of one hundred and eighty days of splendor. Have you anything else?" I smiled and turned from the window as I glanced at my watch.

"Well, I'd like to go on the record as stating that treatment could be successful. Take some time to consider what may be if you would subject yourself to…"

"I hate to interrupt Doc, but I have a quick question. Treatment aside, what are the chances of living? Let us say living through this *without* treatment? A miracle, if you will?" I asked.

Silence filled the room.

His voice broke the silence and provided the answer I expected, "Zero. There's not a chance,"

"Duly noted, Doc. Thank you for your time," I said as I pressed the button on the center of the phone's screen, ending the call.

Six months.

I needed to get busy. I had a wedding to plan.

PARKER

Throughout my latter years of high school, I had hope of receiving a formal education at a University and becoming one of the many professional adults that were gainfully employed in the United States. Upon my graduation from high school, I received an academic scholarship to the University of California San Diego, and eagerly moved halfway across the United States to attend college in the warmth and comfort of southern California.

I had no expectation, however, of completing college and being one of the three and a half percent of the population which was unemployed. In retrospect, attending UCSD and receiving a business degree was probably not in my best interest. Humanities, Fine Arts, Social Science, or one of the many other options would have suited me more favorably from a marketability standpoint in the eyes of a potential employer.

Being eighteen years old, a senior in high school, and making decisions regarding our future as a professional adult should not be allowed. What we believe we want at an early age and what is practical are two totally different things. We are far too young and inexperienced as a senior in high school to understand our future, and far too stubborn to admit it.

After a month of unemployment, I made yet another great decision regarding my future and began seeking employment through advertisements on Craigslist. Although I had avoided the infamous Craigslist killer, I encountered approximately one hundred scams, half a dozen jobs paying less than minimum wage – in cash, and no less than three offers to act as a male prostitute.

I now sat in the law office of Sullivan, Heicht, and Astur waiting on Mr. Astur to see me. This morning, after two solid weeks of searching the same advertisements, a new ad was posted. The manner in which it was drafted made it very interesting and highly unlikely it was a scam. As I glanced around the lavish digs and waited for Mr. Astur, I was quite satisfied this was real. I opened the advertisement on my phone and read it again, making certain of the requirements.

YOUNG ATTRACTIVE EDUCATED MALE WITH HIGH MORAL VALUE

Employer seeks a young educated male who exhibits a high degree of moral value. Applicant must be between 5'-9 and 5'-11, dark hair, and not a drug user. Occasional consumption of alcohol is acceptable.

Must have current driver's license free of infractions. Must be a college graduate. Must be right handed. Must be single, yet willing to entertain the thought of being in a relationship. Must be willing to follow directions and capable of being trusted. Applicant, if accepted, will be required to sign a twenty-four month contract of employment.

Job requires seven days a week of availability.

Compensation package: $80,000/year, company provided transportation, business related expenses, and health insurance.

All interested applicants need apply to the email address as provided. Parties of interest will be interviewed accordingly.

I had read the advertisement multiple times. One thing which troubled me was the lack of description regarding the required skill sets. There was no listed expectation of the employer concerning job performance of the employee. I turned my phone off, placed it into my pocket, and let my imagination run wild.

Actor. Hit man. Bodyguard. Personal assistant.

A personal assistant to a Hollywood type could be very entertaining. I allowed thoughts of working as a personal assistant to Hollywood's finest fill me. Mila Kunis has always been fascinating to me; maybe I would be her assistant. Ashton's schedule probably prohibited him from spending a sufficient amount of time by Mila's side. A personal assistant could solve all of her concerns regarding Ashton's absence. As I closed my eyes and attempted to resurrect an accurate profile of Mila Kunis, I heard footsteps.

I blinked my eyes and looked up from the floor.

Somewhat fascinated, I watched as an extremely attractive thirty-something year old brunette dressed in a dark navy skirt and fitted blazer walked down the hallway until she stood directly in front of me. As she stopped walking, she smiled. I promptly stood and returned the smile. Her dark framed glasses were a superb addition to an otherwise perfect face.

"Parker Bale?" she asked as she raised her eyebrows in what was more than likely false wonder.

"Yes ma'am. I am Parker Bale," I responded as I nodded my head sharply and extended my hand.

She glanced down at my hand and blinked her eyes, "Call me Lisa. Mr. Astur and Mr. Ward are waiting. Follow me if you will."

Gracefully, she turned and began walking down the corridor. As the sound of her heels echoed down the hallway, I followed. Her walk was interesting to say the very least. Each step was as if it were predetermined. It did not appear she was walking by *choice*; it seemed the tile floor was sucking her feet into the exact location they needed to fall into, allowing her to complete perceived walking perfection. I alternated glances between her feet and the hallway in front of us until she stopped.

"Gentlemen, Parker Bale," she smiled as she motioned toward the open door on her left.

I stepped in front of Lisa and into the doorway. Two men, one approximately mid-sixties in age, and one I suspected in his early-forties stood from their respective seats and smiled. The elder of the two was dressed in a business suit and tie. The younger wore jeans and a V-neck T-shirt. As they stood, I walked around the corner of the large table and extended my hand.

"I'm Kenton Ward. My pleasure Mr. Bale," the younger gentlemen said as he shook my hand and smiled.

I turned to face the elder of the two and held my hand in front of my waist as I made eye contact with him. With his lips pursed, he studied my eyes. The few seconds that passed seemed like moments as I waited for his hand to reach mine. The gold specs in his green eyes provided him a certain peculiar presence. As his hand gripped mine, he smiled.

"Hec Astur," he lowered his chin as he spoke.

Heck Ahhhsture. The manner in which the name rolled from his tongue gave him a greater degree of intrigue. As he released my hand he pointed to a chair positioned on the other side of the table.

"Please, have a seat," he said as he motioned to the chair.

"Thank you, Lisa. Close the door if you will," he nodded his head slightly toward the door.

I heard the door close softly as I lowered myself into the ergonomically engineered mesh office chair. As I rested my forearms onto the arms of the chair, I slowly inched closer to the table. Mr. Ward studied me as he lowered himself into his seat and cleared his throat.

"Would you like a beverage? We expect this may take half of an hour," Mr. Astur asked.

"Water if you have it," I responded as I struggled to position my chair the perfect distance from the edge of the table.

"Bottle or glass?" he raised his chin as he asked.

"Bottle please," I responded.

Mr. Astur turned toward Mr. Ward, smirked, and walked to the rear of the large room. As Mr. Astur walked away, Mr. Ward glanced in my direction and smiled while he rubbed his hands together.

"Mr. Bale," Mr. Astur said as he handed me the bottle of water.

Nervously, I held the cold bottle of water in my hands as Mr. Astur walked to the other side of the table and remained standing.

"I represent Mr. Ward from a legal standpoint. I have drafted a contract for the employee which will bind him to the conditions of said contract with Mr. Ward, the employer. In a moment, Mr. Ward will go over his intent regarding employment, but remember," he hesitated as he slid a half inch thick pile of paper across the table.

"The contract governs," he blinked his green eyes and sat down.

"Mr. Ward," Mr. Astur said as he straightened the pile of papers in front of him.

"I'll keep this informal. As you have probably wondered regarding your requested attire for this meeting, I wanted you to be comfortable. Are you comfortable, Mr. Bale?" Mr. Ward spoke slowly, clearly, concisely and properly pronounced every syllable in each prospective word.

"Quite," I nodded as I removed the lid from my bottle of water.

Upon sending my initial email in response to the advertisement, I was advised to *wear whatever you'd be comfortable wearing to meet a woman for a cup of coffee at the Barnes and Noble in the Gas Lamp district* to my job interview. An address and a meeting time were provided. Sitting here now, dressed in Khaki's, a wrinkle-free dress T-shirt, and light blue Sperry's, I felt uncomfortable in the presence of these two men who peered over the table as I took a drink from my unbelievably cold bottle of water.

I smiled as I placed the bottle of water between my legs and slowly screwed the lid onto the top.

"Mr. Bale," Mr. Ward paused and clasped his hands together slowly.

"Chivalry, as they say, is dead. After repeatedly witnessing behavior that is contrary to what I believe is gentlemanly, I have decided to hire an assistant if you will. One who is a natural gentleman. If you were chosen, it would be my intent, in summary, to live vicariously through you as I attempt to mold you into a gentleman. Does or would this type of arrangement interest you?" he asked.

Mr. Ward was a very calm yet full of energy. To watch him, one would think his brain was going a hundred miles an hour. To listen to him speak, he was very matter of fact and appeared astute. He had done nothing to prove his intelligence yet, but I was convinced he was a very intelligent man. As I thought about his question and formed my response, I glanced at Mr. Astur. Slowly, I turned to face Mr. Ward.

"Chivalry, sir, is *not* dead. Although magnanimity isn't commonplace today with the generation of men my age, it certainly exists with some. I would, however, agree we could all take lessons in nobility, generosity, and how to live selflessly. Am I to understand that it is your intent, sir, as is expressed in these contract documents, to form me into a *better* gentleman?" I asked as I picked the pile of documents from the table.

"Impressive response Mr. Bale. I currently have you at one hit and one strike. May I ask why you have chosen to place your bottle of water in your lap?" Mr. Ward asked.

I nodded toward Mr. Astur as I placed the contract onto the table, "Mr. Astur has a coaster in front of him to place his water on. You sir, also have a coaster. When Mr. Astur delivered my water, he did not offer a coaster. As cold as the water is, and considering the temperature in this room, I chose not to chance damaging the top of this wooden table by placing my water on the surface of it."

I smiled, satisfied my answer was impressive. As Mr. Astur nodded and smiled, Mr. Ward unclasped his hands and rubbed his cheeks with the tips of his fingers.

"Why did you choose a bottle of water over a glass when offered?" Mr. Ward asked.

"Both you and Mr. Astur have bottles on your coasters, sir. I was attempting to be polite and trouble free," I smiled as I nodded toward the two bottles of water.

"Trouble free," Mr. Ward repeated as he shook his head.

He pointed to his water, "Have I or has Mr. Astur taken a drink since you've been in the room?"

I thought for a moment. They had not.

"No sir," I responded.

"You requested a bottle of water because we had bottled water? You wanted to be like us?" he asked as he stood from his chair.

"Yes sir," I responded, not knowing what else to say.

"A lure, test, trick, gimmick, whatever you prefer to call it," he paused as he pointed to the bottles of water on the table.

"Drinking water from a bottle is akin to eating beans from a can, cereal from a box, peanut butter from a jar, or drinking wine from a bottle. A beverage is contained in a bottle for shipping and storage. It should remain in the bottle until it is poured into a glass, at which time it could be enjoyed. Do you drink your wine from a bottle, Mr. Bale?" he asked as he slowly walked around the corner of the table.

"No sir," I responded.

"Well, you're batting five hundred so far. Not bad. There's something about you, Parker Bale. Something I like. I have yet to identify what it is, but you have a very good presence about you. Do you want the job?" he asked as he stood beside me and picked the contract up from the table.

"I'm not certain what the job consists of, sir," I looked up as he flipped through the pages of the contract.

He inhaled a slow breath through his nose and exhaled through his mouth.

"You would be provided transportation and money which would be used in finding a woman to develop a relationship with. In a sense, your job is to find the perfect woman *for you*. Preferably once a week, but no less than twice a month, you'd be required to bring her to my home for dinner. All of your dates, meals, transportation, clothes, entertainment, as well as any gifts to her would be provided as a part of the contract at no cost to you. Through the course of developing the relationship, you and I would visit, discussing your intent, direction, feelings, and processes. I would make recommendations to assist you in assuring you always act in a gentlemanly manner," with his hands at his sides he paused, raised the contract, and flipped through the pages.

"Is that it?" I asked.

"In a nutshell, yes. Are you a risk taker, Mr. Bale?" he asked.

"I suppose it depends on the risk, sir," I responded.

His explanation of the job sounded interesting. Driving a company provided car and spending company money. My job would be to eat, drink, and buy gifts for women. Through the course of working, I would also earn eighty thousand dollars a year. It sounded too good to be true.

"I'm going to make you an offer. We have interviewed seven applicants, and have two more scheduled," Mr. Ward flipped through the papers he held, pulled the page from the rear of the contract, and placed it on the table.

"Sign that agreement, Mr. Bale and I will pay you *one hundred thousand* annually. The other benefits remain. This is a one-time offer," he motioned toward Mr. Astur, who reached into his jacket pocket and produced a pen.

As Mr. Astur reached across the table with the pen, I swallowed nervously. One hundred thousand dollars was very tempting, but I had reservations. Not having read the conditions of the contract potentially exposed me to unfavorable legal language. I gripped the bottle of water nervously.

Mr. Ward placed the pen onto the single page of the contract.

"Mr. Bale. Yes or no?" he asked as he motioned toward the pen with his index finger.

"That's it? Taking women on dates and attempting to find my perfect woman. Nothing freaky or crazy?" I asked as I swallowed again.

"There are a few additional conditions and requirements, but no. Nothing freaky or crazy. Finding the right woman, that is all. Yes or no, Parker Bale?" his voice was soft yet stern.

I picked up the pen, removed the lid, and placed the tip onto the page of the contract in the location marked *employee*. I studied the pen.

Mont Blanc.

I looked up at Mr. Ward, "May I ask what interest you have in this?"

"You may. I have not always been a good man, Mr. Bale. In fact, I was quite the opposite. Additionally, I have not always been able, financially speaking, to do such things. Today, I believe I am a good man, and I am quite wealthy. This experiment, if you will, should benefit you, the lady of your choosing, and satisfy me in that I have assisted two people find what it is we all seek," he paused and raised his eyebrows.

"Love," he smiled and pointed to the pen.

"Yes or no?"

I looked down at the page. The greatest rewards in life are provided to those who take the greatest risks.

I signed my name, placed the pen on the sheet of paper, and slid it to my right. Mr. Ward smiled as he scribbled his name beside mine in the location marked *witness*.

"When do I start?" I asked nervously.

"You already have," Mr. Astur responded as he slid a set of car keys across the table.

The blue and white logo in the center of the key was a dead giveaway.

BMW.

"And, now that you're hired, here's the first rule. I am Kenton," Mr. Ward paused and motioned to Mr. Astur.

"He is Hec, short for Hector. We'll address you as Parker. No more Mister this or that. Any questions?" he asked.

I thought about what I may want to ask as I gripped the bottle of water sitting between my legs. As it came to me, I smiled.

"I do have a question," I paused as I raised the bottle of water from my lap and placed it onto the table.

Both men looked at me intently.

"May I have a glass? The thought of drinking from this bottle is repulsive."

PARKER

Simple things please simple minds. I have often wondered if the complexity of my thoughts prevented me from maintaining a higher level of consistent pleasure. I am never particularly sad, but I am rarely overly happy either. Living a simple life full of simple thoughts, according to Kenton, was the key to happiness. Having a mind with the *capacity* of complex thoughts was sufficient to get me in or out of any situation life presented, in his opinion. If my mind was nothing else, it was complex.

I sat at the window, sipped my coffee, and looked out into the courtyard. My first month's wages allowed me to obtain a condominium in San Diego's Old Town. Although portions of southern California were far too hot to allow for a well-manicured lawn, San Diego's climate was perfect for the growth of grass and plant life. I found pleasure sitting at the table and peering through the window at the well sculpted shrubbery which adorned the landscape.

Kenton was a very interesting man, and I found tremendous value in having him as an employer. He had promised over time we would become great friends. To date, he had proven to be handsome, genuine, passionate, unpredictable, and extremely wealthy. He reminded me of a younger version of George Clooney. From what I understood, his home in La Jolla overlooked the ocean; a view everyone wanted and a select few could actually afford.

I had yet to learn much about the background of Kenton Ward, but it was high on my agenda list. I suspected as time passed, Kenton would offer as much detail as he was comfortable allowing me to know. He was a very intriguing man, and having a better understanding of his life's journey interested me greatly.

My schedule for the day was to consist of traveling into San Diego's Gas Lamp District, sit at Barnes and Noble book store, and observe the female patrons for a prospective date. As long as I didn't look beyond the surface of what it was that I was doing for Kenton, everything seemed simple and uncluttered. If I spent time thinking about the intricacies of the contract and his involvement in my life regarding potential relationships, it seemed simply weird.

I walked into the kitchen, rinsed my coffee cup, and grabbed my car keys. I smiled at the thought of spending the day drinking coffee while I observed college aged women – and being paid over eight thousand dollars a month for doing so. In short, I was a player in an odd exercise of human nature development at the expense of Mr. Kenton Ward. My life, for the first time, was going to potentially become interesting.

As I drove to the Barnes and Noble bookstore Kenton recommended, I considered what I would say to any women who may strike my interest. My focus in recent years had not been women, but education; completing my college so as to begin my career amongst the masses in the workforce. My imagination would have never directed me to a career of courting women in a bookstore at the direction of a wealthy gentleman driven by an undisclosed sordid past.

The vehicle Kenton had selected for me was modest by BMW standards, but far from modest by mine. The 3 series coupe with an automatic transmission and leather interior was as nice of a car as I had ever driven. Something about owning and driving it caused me to take extra measures to ensure my actions were in line with one's anticipation of what would be expected of a BMW owner. I was quite certain Kenton had considered this when choosing the car for my use.

After parking the car, I removed my gum wrapper from the console and placed my gum in the wrapper, folded it, and dropped it into my pocket. Chewing gum, for me, was a necessity. Chewing my gum in public, especially while trying to attract a woman, was contrary to what I believed to be in my best gentlemanly interest. I picked up my tablet from the passenger seat, got out of the car, and locked the doors. After a moment of admiring the car, I walked up the sidewalk toward the two-story bookstore which sat on the corner of the block.

The first floor produced not one single available seat. While walking up the wide staircase to the second floor, I noticed several seats open. One was a small table beside what appeared to be a very attractive young lady with what my grandmother would call dishwater blonde hair – and an affection for cooking – or at least reading of it.

"Good morning," I said as I sat at the table on the left side of her.

She turned and studied me intently. As she looked from my toes to the top of my head for the third time, the edges of her mouth curled slightly, revealing extremely white teeth.

"Same," she said over the top of her glasses which rested carefully on the tip of her nose.

"Victoria," she continued as she closed the magazine she was reading.

I looked down at the magazine as she tossed it on the table. *Fine Cooking*. Three others littered the right side of the table and two more sat neatly stacked on her left side. *Bon Appetit*, and *Fine Cooking*. I loved to cook and could talk about cooking all day. In lieu of bringing up the obvious, I opted for a totally different line of conversation.

"Which year was your worst to date, as far as luck goes?" I asked as I opened my tablet and powered it on.

"Excuse me?" she said over her shoulder without looking as she scrunched her nose and flipped through the pages of *Bon Appetit*.

"Luck. Or, well, lack of luck. Let's say bad luck. Which year was your worst for luck?" I grinned.

Dressed in a pair of sheer black pants, a quarter sleeve top, and what appeared to be two inch heels, she looked intelligent with her dark rimmed glasses perched at the tip of her nose. Her eyes appeared to change color from brown to green as her head shifted from side-to-side.

"You're pretty random. 2012 without a doubt, why?" she responded over her shoulder as she lowered the spine of the magazine to meet the table.

"Well, the jade necklace you're wearing. Most people wear jade with the hope of it bringing good luck. I suspected you had either a really bad event, or a really bad series of events which prompted the use of the necklace for luck," I looked up from my tablet as I finished speaking and smiled.

"My my my. Observant aren't you?" she said as she released her magazine and fingered her jade pendant.

"I'm Parker," I smiled.

"First or last?" she asked as she turned and reached toward me with her right hand.

I raised my eyebrows as I extended my hand to meet hers. Before I thought to speak, she began.

"Name? Your name. Is Parker your first or last name?" she asked as she shook my hand.

"First," I smiled.

"It's a good name," she began, nodding her head slowly as she squinted her eyes.

"I like it. I never talk to random people. I can't believe I'm talking to you Parker, but you're cute," she said as she turned her left wrist and glanced at her watch.

I smiled at the thought of her thinking I was cute, and being willing to express it. She certainly wasn't shy. As I admired her hair, she pushed her hands on the edge of the table and began to stand.

"I'm sorry, but I have to work in about fifteen minutes and my current job is in El Cajon," she said as she rose from her seat and began to straighten her mountain of reading material into to a neat pile.

I stood and nervously pressed my sweaty palms against the thighs of my jeans.

"No, Parker. I won't give you my phone number. If that's what you're wondering. Not now, she paused as she looked down at the magazines.

"I'll either see you again or I won't," she said as she picked up the pile of magazines from the table.

"Fair enough. It was a pleasure to meet you," I smiled.

"Likewise," she nodded her head and walked briskly toward the stairs.

As she worked her way down the winding staircase, I smiled at the ease of making conversation with her. Although I realized I may never see her again, I felt satisfied she was very attractive in personality and appearance. As I sat in the chair and looked around the open room, I convinced myself she must be a regular here.

It would stand to reason if she finished looking at three magazines by the time I had shown up, she had arrived early in the morning, probably as the store opened. If she sat upstairs, she had probably come to spend some time here alone, knowing the typical patrons coming and going from the store would never venture up the stairs if they didn't have to.

As I thought of Victoria and what she may do for a living, a brunette at an adjacent table stood and walked to the staircase. Although rather slight, she was attractive and seemed interested in me. The first five steps of her trip down the stairs included an eyeful of me from over her left shoulder.

I raised my hand to my chin and smiled as she disappeared downstairs.

Courting women in the coffee shop was, without a doubt, my calling in life. Without a doubt, this was going to be an interesting summer. In an effort to claim my newfound perch, I left my tablet on the table, stood, and walked toward the staircase. Carefully choosing a few books and a magazine from downstairs just might make me a more interesting option to the single women.

I reached the bottom of the staircase and noticed the thin brunette standing at the counter of the coffee shop. As I turned and walked toward her, she looked over her shoulder and smiled. It wasn't my original intent to attempt to strike up a conversation with her, but considering her expressed interest, I figured I may as well attempt to speak to her.

As I slowly walked her direction, she turned and looked over her shoulder again.

"I saw you met Victoria," she said as I approached, not bothering to turn around and face me when she spoke.

"I did," I paused as I reached for my wallet.

"She doesn't like people. I'm surprised she talked to you. She doesn't talk to anyone. She's in here quite a bit, but she keeps to herself," she said as she picked her coffee up from the counter.

As she turned around, I made mental note of her porcelain like skin and natural good looks. Her hair was cut in what now appeared to be an asymmetrical style, leaving her left side significantly shorter than the right side. For an adult male, I stand a little less than average height, at 5'-10". As she rotated my direction, I realized she was about eight inches shorter than me.

And perfectly beautiful.

"I'm Parker," I muttered nervously.

"Katelyn, Nice to meet you," she smiled and raised her coffee cup in a celebratory fashion.

"Can I help you?" the barista asked.

Overweight, covered in tattoos, and sporting devices in her earlobes which were the size of quarters, the barista stood as a drastic contrast compared to Katelyn. Her visibly dirty hair was cut in a bob and as black as black could possibly be.

"A black cup of coffee, sixteen ounce please," I smiled.

"Pretty basic," Katelyn said as she tilted her head toward the barista.

"$2.76," the barista said.

"I don't like to complicate things," I stated as I handed the barista my newly acquired credit card.

"Carmel macchiato," she said as she raised her cup again, "it's not complicated. It's delicious. Oh my God, you should live a little Parker, it's so good."

And with that remark, she smiled, turned, and walked gracefully toward the stairs. I watched curiously as she worked her way up the steps. When she reached the half-way mark, she turned and smiled over her right shoulder and took a sip from her cup. The shorts she was wearing revealed although thin, her legs were very muscular. My level of interest rose as she reached the top of the steps.

"Can you make that a caramel macchiato?" I asked.

"I've already made you the coffee," she rolled her eyes as she responded, placing the cup of coffee on the countertop.

"I'll pay for both," I nodded, "you still have the card."

"Fine," she snapped as she turned toward the espresso machine.

I grinned at the thought of returning to the upper floor and talking to Katelyn. She was probably the most beautiful woman I had ever seen in person. I stood in wonder if her personality would match her beautiful looks as the barista handed me my freshly made drink.

"What do you want me to do with the coffee?" she asked.

"You can dump it out. Or I suppose you could offer it to someone free of charge," I smiled as she handed me my credit card.

"You always come to book stores to mack on women?" she asked.

"I'm studying," I responded.

"Studying getting laid," she snarled.

I turned and walked up the stairs, eager to speak to Katelyn. As I reached the top of the landing and turned toward my table, she looked up from the book she held and smiled. I smiled in return as I pulled my chair away from the table and lowered myself into it.

The upper floor was sparsely populated. Of the sixteen or so tables situated on the floor, six were occupied, five of which were women. I turned and looked over the handrail and onto the first floor. Primarily filled with women, the first floor was at capacity. A few men sat and read, most of which appeared to be college students. None seemed to be interested in anything but studying.

While turning to face Katelyn again, I raised my coffee cup in the air and waited for her to look in my direction. After a moment, she looked up from her book and grinned.

"Delicious," I mouthed the word silently with my cup held high in the air.

She shook her head and placed the book on the table, marking her page with a small piece of paper. She picked up her coffee cup, yet left her books and purse on the table - indicating she had no intention of actually leaving the book store. As she walked my direction, I took a sip from my drink and fingered the screen of my tablet, fumbling to power it on.

"So, Parker. What's your story?" she asked as she approached the table.

"Story?" I lowered my coffee cup to the table and cupped my hands around it as I looked up and into her eyes.

As she sat down I began speaking.

"I'm an only child. I grew up outside of Cincinnati, Ohio. I was raised by my grandmother and grandfather until my grandfather passed away. I was about six when he died of a heart attack. I have no real recollection of him at all, which isn't surprising. Alone, my grandmother raised me until I graduated high school. I did well in school, received an academic scholarship, and attended UCSD on a full-ride. A few months ago I graduated, and I am now employed as an analyst for a local businessman. I suppose that's about it," I released the cup from my grasp, opened my hands, raised my eyebrows slightly, and waited for a response.

"Where were or are your parents? And what do you analyze?" she asked, smiling.

"They were killed in a car wreck when I was a little less than a year old. And," I paused as I raised my hand to my chin.

"I analyze people. Well. Yes. Let's stick with that. That's about as correct as any other explanation. I analyze people," I smiled as I slowly lowered my hand.

"I'm very sorry about your parents. And, you analyze people? How and why? Tell me how and why. Is that what you're doing now?" she asked as she slowly wrinkled her brow.

"How? Well, I merely collect data, I suppose. What types of people do certain things; I look at where they go, what they do, and why. I gather information and provide it to my employer. I guess calling myself an analyst is a stretch. My employer is more of the analyst. I am the lowly grunt in the field," I chuckled.

"And am I analyzing you now? No. Now I am enjoying the company of a very attractive woman. That's all," I fibbed slightly as I nodded my head in her direction.

"Something about you interests me, Parker. I'm not sure what, but something. Let's keep talking and see what, if anything, we have in common. Sound good?" she smiled as she raked her fingers through the longer side of her hair.

"Sounds great. Yes, start talking, Katelyn. Tell me things about you," I tilted my head slightly and looked along her torso admiringly.

She smiled, slowly raised her eyebrows in an exaggerated fashion, and looked up at the ceiling as she began to speak.

"Well, let's see. I had an interesting childhood. Five sisters. I'm the youngest. The oldest is ten years older than me. My mother and father fell madly in love in college and remain true to each other after all this time," she lowered her chin and took a drink from her coffee cup.

"My father was very strict, but I was rebellious. My sisters, for the most part, lived by his rules. I always made sure to do my best to break or at least stretch them. There's always one kid that's the wild child, and I guess I was that kid," she grinned as she ran her fingers through her hair.

"So, six girls. Wow, that's a lot of estrogen in one home," I said as she crossed her legs and placed her hands in her lap.

"No. Five total. There are five of us. Five sisters. Sorry, I don't have five sisters. We *are* five sisters. Or whatever. There's five. Me and four others. Christi, who's closest to me in age, is a whore," she chuckled.

"That's not nice to say about your sister," I said as I leaned into the back of my chair, waiting for her to expand on the sexual adventures of her sister the whore.

"Well, she is. She can't keep a boyfriend longer than about six weeks," she paused and shook her head slightly.

"If you can even call them that. *Boyfriends,*" she huffed.

"She screws them. And then she leaves them. Call her whatever you want. But she uses them for sex. And she has commitment issues or something. So, in short, she's a whore. A slut. But anyway, tell me more about you," she raised her hands from her lap and pressed her fingers into her temples.

"Do you believe in love, Katelyn?" not certain of why I had asked the question, I sat and waited for her to answer.

She lowered her fingers from her temples and covered her pursed lips with her hands. Her eyes shifted to over my left shoulder and blinked a few times before she began to respond.

"I uhm. Well. Yes. Yes, I do. My parents are proof that it at least *exists*. I think it was or maybe is more prevalent in the older generation, and it's what's missing today in the nation's youth. Kids today don't love, they act. They do whatever they need to do – or what they *think* they need to do to get laid. It's ridiculous," her voice elevated in intensity as she spoke.

She paused and shifted her focus from peering over my shoulder to my eyes.

"I'm all for getting laid. But don't tell me you love me so you can just fuck me. Be truthful; tell me you want to fuck me. Don't cheapen the sex by calling it love. Call it what it is. It's entertainment. It's exciting. It's a great way to kill an afternoon, evening, or night, but it's not love. It's like going to the beach, hiking, or learning how to ride a scooter. It's an event. Love is forever. Fucking is entertainment. Don't even get me started on this subject," she exhaled and shook her head from side-to-side.

"It looks like I already did," I hesitated and took a sip of my lukewarm coffee, "get you started, that is."

"It's a sore subject with me. People saying they love someone, screwing them, and then *screwing them*. Inevitably it ends poorly, Parker. The girl always gets left holding onto some false hope of the most recent douchebag of a boyfriend coming back to her, and he doesn't. He moves on to another victim, screws her, and gives her some bullshit reason for leaving; generally twisting the truth to make it look like it's *her* fault. Fact of the matter is this," she spread her hands about a foot apart and turned her palms upward.

"It never was love, and it was always just about sex. He should have said, *I want to fuck you and walk away without any ties to you. If I have fun fucking you, I may come back and do it again. If I don't enjoy it, don't expect to see me again.* Had he said something like that, she could have made a more intelligent decision – a more fact based decision – and not held onto the hope of him being *the one*. Men. I have little use for them," she clasped her hands together, looked down at my shoes, and shook her head.

"So," I dragged the word along, and hesitated before continuing.

"You want to go on a date?" I asked.

"Seriously? After all of that you want to ask me out?" she chuckled.

"Absolutely," I smiled.

"Just don't tell me you love me and then spend the entire night trying to fuck me," she said as she scrunched her brow into a cartoon like scowl.

"Not a chance," I smiled, "I'm a virgin."

"Whatever," she said as she rolled her eyes and tossed her head to the side.

"I'm serious. My grandmother raised me with old school values," I said flatly as I lifted my cup from the table.

"A date with a virgin. This'll be a nice change. Sounds fun, Parker. When and where?" she asked.

"How does Friday night sound? Say six o'clock or so?" I raised my eyebrows and waited for her response.

"You really a virgin?" she asked, her eyes studying me as she spoke.

I nodded my head sharply, "I certainly am."

"Six o'clock sounds great," she responded.

"How about this," in an effort to make myself seem more interesting and a little on the mysterious side of things, I stood from my chair and picked up my tablet.

"I'll pick you up here at six o'clock on Friday. If everything goes well, we'll exchange numbers and such afterward."

Undeniably surprised, she looked up at me as I picked up my coffee cup.

"Sorry, I have a meeting in a few minutes," I said as I turned my wrist and glanced at my watch.

"Sounds great," she looked up, smiled, and shook her head slowly.

"I'll look forward to seeing you again," I nodded and turned toward the stairs.

As I approached the steps, I dropped my coffee cup into the trash can. Turning to face Katelyn as I pushed my hand into my pocket, I hesitated and held the gaze for a long moment before I stepped onto the first step. When her mouth began to form a smile, I smiled in return, turned, and began to walk down the steps.

Certainly Kenton would be proud of me – considering my accomplishments for the morning. I didn't really understand why, but his approval of my endeavors was important to me. As I stepped through the door and onto the sidewalk, I began to think of what I would tell him regarding having met Katelyn and my morning at the coffee shop.

Kenton had requested my updates be delivered in person. Speaking on the telephone, he advised me, was impersonal. The thought of acting in a manner other than what would be perceived as anything but personal bothered me.

I started the car and typed Kenton's address into the navigation system. As I pulled from the curb, I thought of how I would describe Katelyn to Kenton. Her natural good looks, the asymmetrical haircut, her hatred toward her whorish sister, clear skin, general lack of faith in the male species, and her small yet athletic build.

Imperfectly perfect.

VICTORIA

"Look above the stove, in the pantry," my mother moaned.

"I did mother," I responded as I walked from her bedroom into the living room.

I tried to recall the last time she actually slept in her bedroom. I was probably in middle school. For as long as I could remember, my mother had slept in the recliner in the living room. Basically, she lived in the chair, pointed strategically at the television - which blasted meaningless matter twenty four hours a day.

Without a doubt, painkillers dull all of one's senses, hearing included.

"Can we turn it down a little?" I asked as I walked toward the television.

"I can't hear it now," she said through her fingers as she stretched her hands over her face in agony.

"In the bathroom, under the sink?" she groaned.

"I looked, mother. I've looked everywhere. You're out. Completely," I sighed.

"Go find me *something*. I'll even take Lortab's," she begged in an almost inaudible tone.

My mother had fallen at work when I was in second grade, fracturing several bones in her hip. Her employer was found negligent in court, and was required to settle with my mother financially as well as medically. The end result was a lifelong addiction to pain killers, a short period of unemployment, and a paltry monthly paycheck spent entirely on obtaining more painkillers than the doctor was allowed to prescribe.

Immediately following my birth, my father was killed in a car wreck. My mother never remarried. She claimed he was her first and only love. As I grew older and watched my mother become a drug addict, I often wondered if she was merely wallowing in the grief of her loss by dulling herself senseless with narcotics.

Her medical state didn't allow me to do or see much beyond working. My paychecks primarily kept me in clothes, fed me, and supplemented the amount of painkillers she was prescribed by the doctor.

Her addiction had become her life.

Enabling her had become mine.

"What day is it?" she breathed as she scratched her arms unknowingly.

"It's the fifth," I responded.

Ten more days.

"Oh lord," she groaned.

"I'm going, mother," I sighed as I turned toward my bedroom to retrieve my purse.

Growing up, all I ever wanted was to be a chef. Cooking was something which had always fascinated and satisfied me. I suspect it grew from the necessity to cook for myself at such a young age. In my wildest dreams as a child, I never would have guessed life's destination for me was going to be *here*.

A drug dealer and caregiver to my Barco Lounger dependent narcotics addicted mother.

After assuring her I would return with *something*, I stepped outside and onto the sidewalk. As I walked to my car, I smiled at my recollection of the boy from the book store.

Parker.

The thought of getting to know a boy and developing a relationship was satisfying.

But impossible.

I'd probably never see him again anyway.

If I did happen to see him again, he wouldn't stick around for very long.

They never do.

PARKER

If wealth were measured by the aesthetics of one's living quarters, Kenton Ward was one rich man.

6201 Camino De La Costa.

As the front of my car approached the gate, I stared at the speaker which was carefully hidden in the ornamental stone post on the left side of the brick and stone driveway. As the car came to a stop, I sat and gawked like an idiot; not quite knowing what to do next. A precursory glance toward the trees that surrounded the left side of the entrance revealed a security camera mounted to any ivy covered fence.

I glanced toward where I expected the home to be. From the entrance, the home was well hidden by the stone fence and trees which separated the land in front of the home from the street.

"*Good day Mr. Bale. Mr. Ward is expecting you. Follow the drive to the front entrance of the home, please. Feel free to park in front of the fountain.*"

The voice was pleasant and surprisingly clear.

I stared at the stone post and smiled.

"Thank you," I no more than spoke, and the gate opened automatically.

As I drove slowly along the driveway, I admired the front of the home. I suspect I had some form of preconceived notion regarding what I expected Kenton's home to look like, but what I was seeing cleary wasn't what I had previously expected.

At the end of the drive sat a very spacious two story home with a semi-circular center and straight sides that tapered toward the rear as if they were wings. The circular drive encompassed a large three tier fountain which sat directly in front of the entrance. The front of the home was constructed primarily of glass. A home like this was where I would expect to find Steve Jobs, Mel Gibson, Kobe Bryant, or Tiger Woods.

My heart began to race at the thought of just who Kenton Ward may be.

As I continued to stare at the home admiringly, I unfolded my gum wrapper and dropped my gum into it. A feeling of uncertainty masked my nervous stomach as I stepped from the car and onto the brick drive. As I closed the car door, a man opened the front door of the home and stepped onto the spacious porch.

"It's a beautiful day, isn't it, Mr. Bale? I'm Downes; I assist Mr. Ward in his day-to-day activities," the man said in a soft reassuring tone.

His voice was almost hypnotic.

Without thinking, I pressed the key fob and locked the door of the car. At the sound of the doors locking, Downes spoke again.

"I can assure you your car is safe here, Mr. Bale. Mr. Ward insists on having a secure home. Please come in," he said as he gestured toward the open door behind him.

"Downes?" I asked as I approached the steps.

"That is correct. How has your day been so far, Mr. Bale?" he asked as I walked up the steps and onto the porch.

"Splendid. Thank you," I responded.

Dressed in grey linen pants and a white V-neck designer tee shirt, Downes appeared to be in incredible physical condition. His close cut hair and cleanly shaven face made guessing his age difficult, but I suspected he was in his latter thirties. Stepping through the doorway and into the home revealed a breathtaking display of Kenton Ward's taste.

The home was filled with eclectic furnishings of rich velour, earth tone leather, and animal print. Again, not what I had expected, but it was decorated using extremely good taste.

"Pleasure to see you, Parker. Would you like a sandwich?" Kenton asked as I followed Downes into a large room at the rear of the home.

The exterior wall was constructed of glass and faced the ocean. The view was spectacular. The elevation of the home, in comparison to sea level, was considerably higher. The view was of the ocean, but from this particular location, not of the beach.

In awe, I stood and stared out at the ocean.

"Well?" Kenton strung the word along as he spoke, jokingly.

"Pardon me?" somewhat nervous, I had spoken before I had time to think. He wanted to know about the sandwich, I was sure.

"A sandwich, Parker. You've had one before, I would guess. If not, you should try one. They're quite good; two or more slices of bread with a form of filler in between the slices. Today, it's chicken breast, artichokes, some type of jam, provolone cheese, and what appears to be Romaine lettuce," he paused, rotated the sandwich in front of his face slowly, and looked at it intently.

"On a whole wheat hoagie," he turned to face me and smiled.

"Yes sir. I have had a sandwich before. I'll have one, thank you," I nodded my head slightly as I finished speaking.

"To drink?" Downes asked softly.

"Water. In a glass, please," I smiled.

"The only way it is served," Downes winked, turned, and walked out of the room.

"Stop the *sir* shit, Parker. I'm Kenton. That's all. Understood?" Kenton said in a soft yet stern tone.

"Yes sir," as soon as the word *sir* escaped my mouth, I rolled my eyes.

"My apologies," I paused and shook my head, "Kenton."

"That's better. Are you a golfer, Parker?" Kenton asked as he turned to face the ocean.

He was dressed in khaki shorts, a Polo style shirt, and golf shoes. The shoes made an audible *clacking* noise as he walked across the wooden floor toward the window.

"I have golfed, but I am far from a golfer. I do enjoy the sport," I responded.

"I don't know what type of that jam is, but it's damned tasty," he said as he licked the tips of his fingers.

"Downes, bring me another sandwich, would you?" he spoke in the direction Downes had walked from the room.

"Now, let's sit. Tell me about your day," he said as he turned and walked into the furnished portion of the room.

I studied the furniture, not sure of where to sit.

"Sit wherever you like, Parker. In time, you'll find I'm not the type of person you believe me to be. I'm wealthy, but I'm not a wealthy *prick*. Sit, please," he motioned toward the open room as he spoke.

"It's not so much *you*. I think it's being *here*. It's rather intimidating," I admitted as I walked around the arm of one of the chairs and sat down.

Viewing the home from outside, it was apparent the center section was two stories tall. I assumed the two stories were two stories of living area – two separate floors. Once inside, it was obvious the center of the home was one very, very tall living area. I looked up at the ceiling, which appeared to be thirty feet over my head. As I lowered my head, I looked out once again at the ocean in front of me.

"I can see how it might be. Let me tell you a little about me," Kenton said as he lowered himself into an overstuffed burgundy velvet chair.

He looked around the room as if everything in it was new to him. Slowly, he took every viewable inch of the home into his path of sight. As Downes entered the room with food and beverages, Kenton sighed lightly and nodded in his direction. After leaving the tray containing the food onto a large coffee table positioned between Kenton and me, Downes quietly exited the room.

"My wealth. I didn't deserve it. Hell, I don't deserve it *now*, but I have it. I suspect because I have lived on the other side of the wealthy, and have earned all of what is before you, it allows me to keep myself in check. I don't take my wealth, life, or people for granted," he hesitated and reached for one of the glasses of water.

"At least not *now*. I appreciate all of what I have and what people offer me from my exposure to them. Don't get me wrong," he paused and turned to face me.

"I enjoy *this*," he motioned in my direction and opened his arms toward the room.

"I graduated college and worked in architecture for about ten years. I lived below my means, but appeared - at least on the surface - to be wealthy. I drove a ten year old luxury car, but I kept it spotless. I leased a condo in Old Town. I dressed well. People *assumed* I had money. I allowed them to assume what they assumed, and I used it to my advantage. I manipulated women, had sex with anyone who would allow me to, and never once fell in love. My love, I can easily admit now, was money. My only concern, Parker, was how people perceived me," he shook his head lightly and took a drink from his glass.

"Their perception, albeit an inaccurate one, allowed me to become a horrible person. I cared about nothing and no one but myself. Well, myself and money. I appeared wealthy, worked like a slave, and saved every penny I could. At around that ten year mark, I got an investment tip from a friend on a particular stock. What is now Sirius XM Radio," he stood from his chair, walked toward the windowed wall, and gazed out at the ocean.

"It was 1997. I invested everything I had saved based on this tip. The tip proved to be an accurate one, and through investing, reinvesting, and having the stock split multiple times, I made tens of millions. The money I earned allowed me to make additional investments, and in turn, more money. The money, at least initially, allowed me to become a monster," he said over his shoulder as he continued to peer through the glass.

"I continued to be concerned with nothing and no one but money and myself. The money became a means. I was now able to be the person people had always perceived me to be. I picked women up in clubs, lied to them, wined them, dined them, and had sex with them. I'd immediately move on to another and start over. It was as if I was in some type of contest with myself, and my measure of my success had become fucking various women," he paused, still staring out the window, and took a shallow breath.

"So, one day not too many years ago, Downes and I were eating in a restaurant. It was right after he returned from Afghanistan and went to work for me, 2005 I believe. The woman sitting beside us in the restaurant was alone and attractive, so naturally we began to talk. Through the course of talking I learned she had been a victim of sorts," he placed his hands on his hips, hesitated and looked upward.

"One night in a bar in Mission Hills, she met a man. One thing led to another, and they ended up at her place. She said he convinced her he had tremendous interest in her as a person and a potential mate. Destiny, he told her. Soul mates or some other ridiculous shit, I don't recall. At any rate, that night, they had sex. Her efforts to contact the man after that first night were unsuccessful, he provided her with a fake phone number. Imagine that."

"A month later, she missed her period. A pregnancy test revealed what she already feared. Nine months passed, she gave birth to a daughter, and now raises the girl alone. Some might say her life was ruined. Others, I suppose, could look at it as a blessing or a gift. It didn't settle well with me. She is raising a child who will never know her father. She'll never have a family in a conventional sense. The child becomes the victim, and for what reason?" he turned from the window, walked toward the burgundy chair, and sat down.

I sat quietly and listened as Kenton Ward began to become human.

"Her story wasn't awful, and it certainly wasn't all too devastating. I had no ties to her or her daughter and I've heard far more saddening stories many times. But Parker, for whatever reason, her story was what I needed to hear when I needed to hear it. Here we had a woman who had fallen for a man who wasn't necessarily truthful with her. As a result, she had been forced to raise her daughter alone. At that particular moment, as we sat in the restaurant, I thought about her misfortune. And something within me changed. A spiritual awakening, hell I don't know. *Something*," he turned toward me and smiled as he placed his empty glass onto the coffee table.

"Have a sandwich before the bread hardens. I'm almost finished," he said as he reached for one of the plates.

I reached for the remaining plate, placed it on my lap, and lifted the sandwich to my mouth.

"Wow. This is amazing," I said after I swallowed my first bite of the sandwich.

"I think it's the jam. Karen is quite a cook. She's young and struggles with maintaining a diverse menu, but she can cook like no other," he chuckled as he took a bite of the sandwich

"At any rate, on that day, for whatever reason, something within me changed. I attempted to make amends with everyone I harmed in my wake of being me. In doing so, I learned a lot about myself, Parker. Not all of which, I might add, was good. The end result, you might ask? I haven't been with a woman since. It's been almost ten years, I guess. I had told myself I'd forfeit all of this, everything..." he paused, motioned around the room, and took another bite of his sandwich.

"My belongings, wealth, as well as myself to the woman I love and only if I truly loved her. I just had to find her or allow her to find me. In *that* regard, I've tossed my respective hands in the air. For me, the search is over. In recent years, I've decided to live my life in a manner I believe to be kind, considerate, and caring. Along the way, I've selected a few people to befriend, help, or guide, if you will. You, Parker, are one of those people," he placed the uneaten portion of his sandwich on the plate and stood from his chair again.

"Parker, life is like a Texas Hold 'em Tournament. The poker tournament, have you seen them?" he turned to face me, waiting for some form of acknowledgement.

"I've seen them on ESPN. The tournaments, yes," I nodded as I wondered what the similarities were, at least in his mind.

Kenton began to pace in front of the window as he spoke.

"Everyone gets two hole cards. Only you get to see these cards. Everyone has an opportunity to bet, check, raise, or fold. To bet is to place money on your belief that you'll win. To check is to say, *so far, I like what I see, but I want to see more.* It cost nothing to check. To fold is to say, *based on what I've seen, I give up. This isn't worth my time or effort.* Three more cards are dealt. *The flop.* Everyone gets to bet, check, raise or fold. Then, another card is dealt. *The turn.* Bet, check, raise, or fold again. Then, the last card is dealt. *The River.* Bet, check, raise, or fold. It's a simple game."

"The tournament, like life, starts with a wide assortment of people. Wannabe's, hacks, the hopeful, the desperate, the one or two who inevitably lied or fumble-fucked their way into the room, the ones who are slowly learning, a few who know actually how to play – but not necessarily well, and then there's *the one.* The one person who has it all figured out. He has every potential option, equation, and scenario tucked away in the back of his mind. Based on experience, their understanding of people, and some simple mathematics, he or she will kick the respective ass of everyone else, Parker."

"Now, it's down to you and him. He gets his hole cards and checks. You look at yours. A pair of aces. After the ace, nine, deuce flop, he checks. You wonder why he's even there. You're sitting on three aces. On the turn, another deuce, and he goes all in. Hell, he shoves a million three hundred and fifty fucking thousand dollars into the center of the table. He's *that sure. What's he thinking,* you ask yourself. And you study the cards. You wonder. You don't see it. All you see is your three aces. He must have *something.* You can't see it. *Fuck it,* you say. You go all in. Say a million one. Everyone gasps. They can't believe it. Over go your cards, and you realize that the deuce you saw on the flop wasn't the only deuce on the table. You missed the deuce on the turn. And he's holding the other two. For some reason you didn't see it. You forgot to eat breakfast. You had one too many martinis for lunch in the lounge. Your girlfriend called you the night before and said *I wanted some space.* Your ingrown toenail hurts, who fucking knows. But you missed it. The river card is your only hope, and here it comes…an eight of hearts. You lost. He won. You missed a small detail and it cost you," he continued to pace and look out at the ocean.

"The details, Parker. Details. You have to pay attention to the details. They'll be the death of you if you don't. And you have to know when to shove your cards to the center of the table and say, *I give up.* There's no shame in it. All the winners do it, and they do it regularly. The unintelligent, the dreamers, and the unknowing don't," he hesitated, and took a slow breath.

"And as a result they lose." he breathed.

"Conversely, you must know, and *know you must,*" the tone of his voice changed to stern as he stopped pacing, turned, and shook his finger toward me.

"When to hold your cards close to your chest and say, *I'll risk it all.* Being so certain that what you're holding is *right.* That it is, without a doubt, the clear winner. So sure that you're willing to risk it all, everything you have, *knowing* you have a winner in your hands."

"In life, know when to *check.* It cost nothing to see what little additional life has to offer. Know when to *fold.* It's when life's dealt you a hand that just isn't worth the risk. And know, Parker, when to hold your cards close to your chest and risk it all. Don't ever be afraid to go *all in,* as long as you believe you're holding a clear winner."

I sat in the chair and stared at him in admiration. He was a very intelligent man with very sound advice. Life had most definitely dealt me a winning hand when Kenton decided to employ me. I didn't want to disappoint him, and hoped that he would understand if I ever made decisions that were contrary to what he believed was best. I looked down at my empty hands and realized I had finished my sandwich.

"So, tell me about your morning. I took control of the conversation earlier and didn't even let you speak. I'll do that if I'm allowed. Just tell me to shut my mouth if I do it again," he grinned, slowly walked to the chair, and sat down.

"Well," I squirmed in my seat as I considered where to start.

"Don't worry about what you say or how you say it, Parker. Just talk. We're simply two guys discussing the events of our day. It'll make me far more comfortable when you become at ease speaking with me, that's for damned sure," he rested his elbow on his thigh, lowered his chin into his hand, and raised one eyebrow slightly.

I smiled.

He laughed.

And I became a little more comfortable.

"Well, I went to the bookstore in Old Town. The two-story Barnes and Noble we discussed. I met a few girls, and I have a date with one of them Friday," I paused, waiting for his praise.

"Her name? The one you're taking on a date, that is," he asked.

"Katelyn."

He nodded his head slowly as he took the name into consideration.

"That's a good name. Is she in school? Does she work?" he asked.

I thought of what Katelyn and I had discussed. We had talked about love, sex, her hatred of most men, and her whore sister, Christi.

"I'm not certain, we didn't discuss it," I responded.

"So," he hesitated and lifted his chin from his hand.

"You're going on a date with someone you virtually know nothing about?" he asked as he stood from his chair.

"Well, she has four sisters, one of which she perceives as being a whore. She believes in fucking, but not so much in love. She's leery of men, and thinks they are deceptive and untruthful. Her parents have been together since…" I paused and thought as Kenton walked toward the window.

"Well, I'm not sure how long, but for a long time. She believes they're in love. She said she believed in love, just that most men were more interested in sex than love. She said they threw the *word* love around in an effort to obtain sex."

"So, you're going on a date with someone you know virtually nothing about?" he asked again.

With his hands in the pockets of his shorts, he turned from facing the ocean and stared at me over his shoulder.

"I, uhhm. I suppose that's accurate. I know very little about her. She was, however, attractive," I responded.

"Was she? What about her was attractive?" he asked as he turned around completely.

I thought about her walking up the stairs while I waited for my coffee.

"She was very thin, but muscular. Her skin was smooth and olive colored. She had beautiful hair and equally beautiful features. Possibly the most attractive female I have ever spent time talking to," I grinned, pleased at the fact that Katelyn was as beautiful as she was.

"It's all too easy for us to become attracted to someone's *appearance*. We're then forever blind to *whom* they actually are. Ask yourself this, Parker. If you had not actually had an opportunity to see her, and had spoken to her as she sat behind a mirrored glass, what would be your thought of her?" he lowered himself into the chair and sat in wait for my response.

I considered what he had asked. I tried to eliminate my thoughts of her beauty. Had I truly walked into an empty room and had a conversation with her, but not seen her, what would I think? My recollection of what she spoke of – her sisters, thoughts regarding love, and her take on sex was fairly clear. I began to recall what she said regarding sex.

I'm all for getting laid. But don't tell me you love me so you can just fuck me. Be truthful; tell me you want to fuck me. Don't cheapen the sex by calling it love. Call it what it is. It's entertainment. It's exciting. It's a great way to kill an afternoon, evening, or night, but it's not love. It's like going to the beach, hiking, or learning how to ride a scooter. It's an event. Love is forever. Fucking is entertainment.

I started to grin.

"Well, we wouldn't be going on a date, that's for sure," I responded, still grinning.

I was becoming a student of Kenton Ward.

"How easily we become distracted by beauty. It's quite sad. If only we could close our eyes and become attracted to what's on the inside," he said flatly.

Quietly, Kenton looked around as if he expected some form of response or answer from within the room. He didn't appear to be frustrated with me, but the fact that he had stopped speaking made me wonder what he was thinking.

"Friday?" he asked blankly as he turned to face me again.

"Friday," I responded, half ashamed of my having asked Katelyn on a date.

"Well, I have some errands to get done today; I should probably start pretty soon. If you're in the neighborhood and she's bored, stop by Friday. With Katelyn, that is. I'll be here. Actually, I'm anxious to meet her," he said as he stood from the chair.

"I'll plan on it," I responded as I placed my hands on my knees.

"In the event you do come here, we're *friends*. No need to muddy the waters with explanations of employment. Agreed?" he paused, waiting for my approval.

"Agreed," I responded as I stood.

I rose from the overstuffed chair I had been buried in for the length of our conversation. During my visit, Kenton had asked little of me, yet offered considerable wisdom in the form of advice. He wasn't the person I expected him to be. I remained quite nervous in his presence, and reserved hope this would change in time. As the cleats of his golf shoes echoed down the hallway toward the front door, I followed anxiously.

"You should live every day," Kenton paused as he reached for the door handle, "as if you're going to die at midnight."

Leisurely, he pulled the door open.

"Ask yourself throughout the course of each day, *if this were my last day on this earth, would I do anything different?*"

"I've been saying that since I was in college. Only in the last decade did I truly start applying it. Have a nice afternoon, Parker. I hope to see you Friday," he said as he extended his right hand.

I shook his hand and nodded, thinking about what he said. *If this were my last day on this earth, would I do anything different?* At a loss for words, I stepped onto the porch, turned to face him, and thought.

"Yes," I said.

And, as Kenton Ward's mouth slowly formed itself into a grin of accomplishment, I quietly turned and walked to my car.

PARKER

Having a job that wasn't necessarily a conventional one left me considerable time to think. Thinking, for me, hasn't always been a healthy thing. I tend to think, rethink, and overthink issues if left with enough time. Being decisive is not one of my strengths. Through the course of the morning, I had changed my mind no less than four times regarding Katelyn and our date.

Although I couldn't be certain, I began to wonder if some of my indecisiveness was a result of a desire to please Kenton. I desperately wanted acceptance from him, and couldn't convince myself he was pleased with my decision to take Katelyn on a date. He had, however, asked that I bring her to his home on Friday. This, in itself, was enough to cause me to second guess my second guessing.

Sitting in the kitchen and staring out into the courtyard, I tried to relax and think of things other than Katelyn and Kenton. My mind became a scrambled mess of thoughts as I sipped my cup of coffee and gazed out the window at what must have been one of San Diego's tallest palm trees. Half way into my mental efforts to guess the height of the tree, I decided to give up. Left wondering and somewhat frustrated, I stood and walked to the bathroom.

I suspect I pluck my eyebrows more than most people. I will never actually know if it actually provides me any form of real relaxation or a means of solving problems, but I like to think it provides *something*. During a few of my college exams, I plucked my eyebrows into nothingness.

Generally, I perform the task while I am making decisions. Or thinking. Or thinking about making a decision.

Standing in front of the mirror, tweezers in hand, I attempted to resolve the issue of the palm tree.

If a telephone pole is typically forty feet tall, and they are buried ten percent of the length plus two feet, that would leave thirty-four feet of the pole exposed.

Pluck. Pluck.

The tree is thirty three percent taller than the pole.

Pluck. Pluck. Pluck.

If the pole beside the tree is typical, the tree is forty three feet tall. That would be if the pole is typical.

Pluck.

Assuming typical length for the pole, my math is correct. Forty-three feet.

Pluck. Pluck. Pluck.

Pluck.

Too many variables. Far too many.

Pluck. Pluck.

What if Kenton really wants me to step aside and not take Katelyn on a date?

Surely he would have expressed his concerns. If nothing else he would have spent some time discussing it.

He did not.

Pluck. Pluck. Pluck. Pluck.

He wants me to take her to meet him. That's the reason he hired me.

He wants me to do what is right. Regardless of who Katelyn is and why we're on a date, the right thing to do is to proceed with the plan.

Pluck.

I need to do what is right.

Pluck.

Yet.

I need to know when to fold my hand.

Pluck. Pluck. Pluck.

When to forfeit.

Pluck.

Now is not the time.

I need to continue, proceed, move forward. If there is a lesson to learn, I will learn it. I won't make the same mistake twice.

I looked at my reflection in the mirror. I rotated my head slowly and focused on my eyebrows. The light above the mirror provided sufficient illumination to support what I already assumed.

Eyebrow perfection.

PARKER

The passage of time has always been something I have found fascinating. Seconds. Minutes. Hours. Days. Weeks. Months. Seasons. Years. Decades. Lifetimes.

Through the course of college, time passed at various speeds. Generally speaking, it was all too quickly. There never appeared to be enough time to get the work completed that was before me. After I had graduated, it seemed as if it was no more than a year ago when I started.

Time passes at a constant rate. It never changes. A second is always a second. Sixty of them make a minute, and sixty minutes make one hour.

Always.

Our perception of the passage of time, however, changes. I believe when I am anxious of the arrival of a particular event, time seems to pass very slowly. If I allow myself to become consumed by smaller events preceding the larger event, time seems to pass more quickly.

In short, I have concluded thinking - or reasoning - creates the illusion of time passing slowly. Mindlessness allows us to fly through the days and nights as if they never existed. One may stand to reason, and I certainly do, that a thoughtful person lives a lifetime equal to three or four of that of a mindless couch potato.

Fascinating.

"Oh my God, It seems like this day just *appeared*. You know, it was here like…well, *boom!*" Katelyn tossed her hands in the air to demonstrate the explosion.

"It sure arrived quickly, didn't it?" I turned my head and smiled, knowing it seemed like an eternity.

I turned the corner onto Camino De La Costa. As I proceeded up the street, Katelyn's jaw noticeably dropped. Sitting in the passenger seat with her mouth open, staring at the homes along the road, she spoke.

"Oh. My. God."

6201. Here we are.

Slowly, I turned into the entrance of Kenton's home.

"Breathtaking, aren't they?" I said as I came to a stop beside the stone post.

The gate slowly began to open.

"Good evening Mr. Bale," a familiar voice came from the speaker.

"*Mr. Bale?* Just who the hell are you?" Katelyn asked.

"Just a friend of Kenton's," I responded, smiling.

Katelyn continued to gawk at the front of the home as I drove up the drive toward the fountain. It was almost dark, and it appeared every light in the home was illuminated. The front of the home was not only well lit from the inside, the outside had a considerable amount of landscape and architectural lighting on the surface of the exterior walls. Every irregular surface cast a long shadow upward, creating an illusion of depth and distance.

As the car came to a stop at beside the fountain, Downes stepped onto the porch.

"What's your last name?" I whispered as I reached for the door handle.

"Excuse me?" she asked.

"Your last name, what is it?" I asked as I held the door handle and waited to open the door.

"Uhhm. Moss," she responded.

I nodded as I opened the door. As I walked around the front of the car toward Katelyn's door, Downes nodded his head and smiled. When Katelyn stepped from the car, I slowly began walking toward the porch.

Staring up toward the large windows, Katelyn stumbled on the drive as she walked beside me. As she stumbled, I caught her arm in my hand, steadying her stance.

"Downes," I paused.

"Miss Katelyn Moss," I continued as I stepped onto the bottom step.

"The pleasure is mine, Miss Moss. Please, follow me. Mr. Ward is perfecting his ability to putt," Downes said as he turned to face the front door.

"Oh my God," Katelyn gasped as she stepped into the hallway.

We followed as Downes walked toward the rear of the home. As we approached the windowed wall which faced the ocean, Downes turned to the right and stopped in front of two large French doors. As he opened one of them, I noticed Kenton's shadow on a putting green below the patio.

"Mr. Ward. Mr. Bale and Miss Katelyn Moss here to see you," Downes said sharply from the elevated deck of the patio.

Kenton spoke as he turned to face us.

"My apologies," he said as he began to walk from the putting green toward the steps that led to the patio.

"But the game of golf, Miss Moss is lost or won right here," he gestured toward the green.

"On the putting green," he began to walk up the steps, using the putter jokingly as a cane.

"Everyone gets *on* in two or three strokes," he paused and extended his hand toward Katelyn.

"And they'll four putt their way into a loss. I have vowed not to step onto another course for as much as a glass of tea until I can have a sub-par round at Torrey Pines' south course. I need practice. Miss Moss, pleasure to meet you, I'm Kenton Ward," he smiled as she shook his hand.

Her mouth still noticeably agape, she silently shook his hand.

"May I call you Katelyn?" Kenton asked.

"Yes. Yes sir, you may," she stumbled.

Kenton nodded and turned to face me. He raised his hand and slapped me on the shoulder lightly.

"Parker, you rarely stop and visit. Let's change that, shall we?" he chuckled.

"I'll do my best, Kenton," I grinned.

"Katelyn, do you drink tea?" Kenton asked as he turned and began to walk toward a wrought iron table positioned on top of the patio.

"Yes, I do," she responded.

Kenton nodded toward Downes, who disappeared quietly through the French doors.

"Please, sit down," Kenton motioned toward the chairs which surrounded the table.

Kenton smiled as I pulled a chair from the table and waited for Katelyn to sit. After she sat, I lowered myself into the chair beside her. Kenton leaned his putter against the handrail of the patio pulled out a chair across the table from us. As he sat down, he looked down at his shoes.

"It seems I never take these damned things off. I spend all of my spare time on this damned green, Parker. You'd think I had some vested interest in the game. Nothing could be farther from the truth," he grinned as he looked up.

"I've never been," Katelyn paused and turned from staring out at the ocean to face Kenton, "golfing that is."

"Well, it's a frustrating sport to say the least. So, Parker, what have you two filled your evening with?" Kenton asked as he leaned into his chair and faced me.

"Well. We ate dinner, drove around and talked for a bit, and decided to come visit you. To end the evening on a relaxing note," I gestured toward the ocean as I spoke.

"What was for dinner?" Kenton asked.

"Oh my God. We went to Rockin' Baja Lobster," Katelyn stammered, obviously still excited from my choice of the restaurant.

"You must have planned that, Parker. Getting into that place on a Friday night is impossible without a reservation. The lobster corn chowder is a must. One of my favorite places," Kenton smiled.

"Oh my God. We *had* the chowder. It was so good. And a Cortez Bucket. It was so good," Katelyn sat up in her chair and clasped her hands together as she spoke.

"What was in the Cortez? I always get the Baja Bucket; chicken, beef, shrimp, and lobster. I can't seem to stray from it. Maybe it's partly that I know I'll leave satisfied," Kenton grinned and rubbed his palms together feverishly as he waited for Katelyn to respond.

"Oh my God. It was lobster and uhhm," Katelyn looked up and pressed her fingers against her cheeks.

The French door opened and Downes stepped to the patio with a pitcher of tea and three glasses on a tray. Quietly, he placed the serving tray onto the table in front of us, poured three glasses, and turned away.

"Crab. Lobster, crab, and shrimp. Oh my God, it was so good," Katelyn said as she reached for a glass of tea.

If she says 'oh my God' or 'it was so good' again, I may vomit.

"It's peach tea. Karen made it this afternoon. I enjoy it. Tell me what you think, Katelyn," Kenton said, winking in my direction as Katelyn raised the glass to her mouth.

As Katelyn lowered the glass onto the table, she smiled.

"Oh my God," she said, licking her lips, "it is so good."

As the bile rose in my throat, I was grateful that we had eaten seafood for dinner, and not Mexican food. I felt somewhat embarrassed about Katelyn's immature behavior and repeated responses to Kenton's questions. I glanced at my watch. 8:35.

This night couldn't end quickly enough.

I had not devoted much time to dating women compared to most men, I was certain. I began to realize why as Katelyn babbled. As she continued to speak, I realized her voice was becoming more and more distant. *Muffled.* I was doing with her what I used to do with Mrs. Best in third grade.

I was ignoring her; building a mental dam of sorts. It prevented her voice, ideas, or opinions from littering my mind. The act of mentally eliminating her from existence was all but second nature to me.

Mrs. Best was my teacher in third grade. Her voice was annoying, her opinions weren't worth hearing, and her statements regarding most anything were inaccurate at best. I learned to block her voice from being heard, and as I perfected the process, I often found myself in trouble. Once, to my surprise, I had blocked out an entire hour of her class. At the end of class, she called on me to respond to a question she had asked. I didn't even realize she was speaking at all until another student nudged me, bringing me out of my semi-comatose state.

"Parker. You weren't paying attention. You were drooling," Mrs. Best said.

All of the children in the class snickered and laughed.

I raised my hand to my lip.

Dry.

"I *was* paying attention," I responded as I lowered my hand to the desk, frustrated she tried to embarrass me.

"What was the discussion?" Mrs. Best asked as she glanced at the clock.

I looked at the clock. I had blocked out the entire one hour class. Only three minutes remained. I glanced to my left. Jessica looked at me and smiled as she covered her mouth with her hand.

"*Synonyms, antonyms, and homonyms,*" Jessica whispered.

"Synonyms, antonyms, and homonyms," I looked around the room as I responded.

"Impressive. Can you explain to the class the differences between them?" Mrs. Best asked.

Knowing there wasn't another kid in the class that could answer this question accurately; I thought of what my grandmother had taught me in the countless hours of studying at home.

"A synonym is a word which means the same thing as another word. *Laugh and giggle.* An antonym is a word that is the opposite of another word. *Big and small.* And a homonym is a word that sounds like another word but means something different," I paused and thought for a moment.

I looked at Mrs. Best and smiled, "I went *to* the store. *Two* plus two is four."

As Mrs. Best looked at me in disbelief, the buzzer sounded, ending class. As I stood from my chair and gathered my books, I looked at Jessica and smiled. As she smiled in return I felt warmth inside my chest. Jessica was nice and her hair reflected the sun instead of absorbing it. Throughout middle school, I liked that about her.

"Isn't that right, Parker?" Kenton's voice was barely audible.

I blinked my eyes and glanced at my watch. 9:05. I had lost thirty minutes. I processed what Kenton had asked and thought of a safe response.

"Absolutely," I chimed, smiling.

I turned toward Katelyn, wondering what she and Kenton had talked about for thirty minutes. Her hair absorbed every bit of light from the patio. A dull, dirty ball of asymmetrical blackness atop her head, she looked my direction and smiled.

Unlike when Jessica smiled at me in school, I didn't feel the warmth inside. I didn't feel that her smile offered me something to look forward to. In fact, it had, in a short time, become irritating. I focused on her once beautiful eyes.

I felt cold inside.

It was time I ended this date, and take Miss Katelyn Moss home.

Wait a minute.

Katelyn Moss.

Kate Moss.

My date for the night shared the same name as the crack smoking, former, not-so-super supermodel.

I should have known.

I sat and recalled what was sure to become some very valuable words of one Kenton Ward. *And, you have to know when to shove your cards to the center of the table and say, 'I give up.' There's no shame in it. All the winners do it, and they do it regularly. The unintelligent, the dreamers, and the unknowing don't.*

And as a result they lose.

The time had come for me to shove my cards to the center of the table and give up. I needed to fold this particular hand, and do so in as graceful as a manner as I could develop. I needed to get her away from here and do it away from Kenton, minimizing my exposure to his scrutiny.

I turned to Katelyn.

"You want to go to Belmont Park and ride the Mission Beach roller coaster? The Giant Dipper?" I asked.

"Oh my God. That sounds awesome. You want to go, Kenton?"

I turned toward Kenton and waited for what would be his certain response in the form of *no*. Without a doubt, he had much more important things to do on a Friday night than accompany us to Belmont Park. As he stood from his chair and straightened the fabric of his shorts, I attempted to disguise the grin developing on my face.

"I'd love to," Kenton responded.

As the bile once again rose in my throat, I began to realize the value in being more cautious of whom I may ask out on a date, and less eager to simply fill a void in a schedule on a calendar. Muffled voices in the background continued. I was blocking her out again – a failed effort to make her disappear. I stood from my chair and followed as Katelyn and Kenton walked into the house. I had yet to develop a single plan of how to rid myself of Katelyn and do so with any degree of grace. I decided to allow the night to unfold and look for any opportunity that may present itself.

Katelyn turned and walked into the hall bathroom, giggling. As she closed the door, I turned toward Kenton and made eye contact for the first time of the night. Somewhat embarrassed, I stared, not quite knowing what to say.

"Oh my God," he whispered mockingly.

"I know," I sighed in return.

"So, when is the second date?" he chuckled as he reached down and removed one of his golf shoes.

"There won't be one," I responded.

"Here's my advice, Parker," he paused as he pulled the shoe from his other foot.

"Be delicate, kind, and remain friendly with her. Explain in the best manner you are able that she merely doesn't fit the mold of what you seek in a mate. She won't like it, but she'll understand. Be clear. Women typically maintain or develop hope if you aren't one hundred percent clear with your intent. Be concise. And by all means, do so after this night is over," he said, his golf shoes dangling from his fingers.

I nodded in acknowledgement as Kenton finished speaking. I realized as he turned to walk away although he may look at this as an employer employee relationship, I – in many respects – was beginning to view it as somewhat of a father son relationship.

The thought of which provided me with comfort.

And pain.

PARKER

Life is far more abrasive in experiencing the individual components than the sum itself. I liken it to the ingredients that make up a recipe. For instance, grilled beef tenderloin in Cabernet sauce first requires balsamic vinegar, garlic, rosemary, peppercorns, olive oil, and salt for the steak marinade. Individually, or standing alone, none of these ingredients are very palatable.

The steaks, once soaked overnight in this marinade and grilled, clearly define how an herbed, spiced filet mignon should taste. Regardless of the quality of the latter prepared Cabernet sauce, the steaks are merely chunks of grilled meat without the initial marinade. The sum of ingredients will develop something to be enjoyed by all who partake in the meal. Individually, the ingredients are repulsive at best.

I believe life can be compared to cooking in many respects. We know not to add vanilla to spaghetti sauce. In a batch of our favorite cookies, however, it may be quite tasty. Additionally, a slice of bell pepper which may work well in a salad would be out of place in a German chocolate cake. I feel I need to be cautious of the people I permit into my life no differently than I would be careful of the ingredients I would include in a recipe. I suppose a good recipe for life would be to allow nothing into it, knowingly at least, which is bitter.

It's disappointing we aren't able to simply spit people out that don't taste well.

"Maybe I had one too many glasses of wine. I'll do better next time. I really enjoyed myself," she said sheepishly.

"It's not any of those things. You didn't do anything *wrong*. It's just that," I paused and tried to think of something to say that would satisfy us both.

"It's just that I, well, I'm *different*. I desire certain things in a woman, and you don't possess the qualities I require. To continue wouldn't be fair to you or to me either one," as I finished speaking, I realized I hadn't really offered much explanation.

"How would you know I don't have what you want? We spent one night together. *One*. Give me some time," she pleaded, her eyes glistening from the tears that began to well.

"Time won't change anything. I like you Katelyn. It's simply that, well…" I hesitated, realizing this wasn't going as easily as I expected it to.

"There's not a future in us continuing to see each other on a romantic level." I said, my voice trailing to an almost whisper.

Satisfied, I exhaled and picked my cup of coffee up from the table.

It was immediately apparent Katelyn had no intent on continuing to attempt anything with me, romantic or otherwise. I had, for whatever reason, become something she found tasteless; and she began to spit me out.

"No future on a romantic level? *Romantic?* Fucking fine. Just fine," she barked as she stood from her chair.

"I bet if you fucked me you'd be singing a different song, you rich little prick. You'd be begging me to stay. You don't know what you're missing you fucking douche," she snapped.

Immediately Katelyn turned, walked toward the stairs, and stopped as she gripped the handrail. Standing there, the handrail in one hand and her purse in the other, she turned to face me. Over her left shoulder she stared my direction, as if there was something else she wished to say, but was incapable. Her lip quivered.

And she began to softly cry.

The part of me that felt at least a portion of what she was feeling wanted to stand and comfort her. The sensible part of me told me to remain seated and look through her and not directly at her. As I peered over her shoulder at the light fixtures suspended from the ceiling, I watched her blurry silhouette slowly turn and walk down the stairs.

As I noticed the frame of the front door open and close against the glass storefront, I allowed my eyes to become focused again. Quite some time had passed since Katelyn and I had begun our conversation, and it appeared several people had joined us on the upper platform of the bookstore.

And, seated at the table beside the stairs, where I had stationed myself a few days before, was Victoria – the girl who reportedly doesn't like people – and talks to no one. Sitting there, amongst an equally tall pile of magazines and a few books, she looked the same as she did the first day I saw her.

Beautiful.

Yet.

Her physical beauty wasn't her most attractive quality, at least not at this point. Something about her being a bit of a recluse, not talking to anyone, and *not liking people* made her very interesting to me. It wasn't that these things made her *more* attractive, because they really didn't. They did, however, create wonder on my part. Not knowing who she was and why she chose to be alone made her far more intriguing of a person. This intrigue caused me to stare.

The stare allowed me to become mentally lost in wonder.

And, as I become mentally lost, I began to relax.

Lost in thoughts of Victoria and now in a blissful state of relaxation, I felt something heavy slipping from my right hand.

"Oh shit!" I howled as the coffee cup fell from my hand and bounced on the table top.

As fate would have it, the cup bounced, landing on its side. As it landed, the lid snapped from the top. Immediately, I found out how much of a mess a few ounces of coffee make on a clean table. Frantic, I scanned the upper floor, unsuccessfully, for a condiment bar. With all eyes trained on me – no doubt from my choice to scream expletives in a quiet bookstore – I cupped my hands around the edge of the spill. Looking down at the caramel colored ocean, I took a deep breath and looked up slowly.

Victoria.

"Here, let me help," she smiled as she dropped a handful of paper napkins into the middle of the spill.

"Thank you," I sighed.

Sweeping the napkins in a circular motion, I quickly cleaned the mess from the table. Victoria followed behind me as I picked the pile of wet napkins up, wiping the table further with a rag.

"I didn't see a condiment station up here," I said as I stood from my chair.

"There isn't one. I ran downstairs and got these. What happened?" she asked.

"I knocked my cup of coffee over. Not paying attention, I guess," I shook my head slightly from side to side and stepped toward the trash can.

"It looked to me like you just *dropped* it," she chuckled.

"Pardon me?" I said over my shoulder as I released the napkins into the trash.

"Dropped it. As in *dropped*. You were holding it," she said, her hand held at arm's length, cupping her palm into a circle.

"You looked like you were in a daze. Maybe you were in shock from the girl that just dumped you, I don't know. But the cup just fell out of your hand. I watched it happen. It was in slow mo," she said jokingly, acting as if she were dropping a cup from her hand as she spoke.

"She didn't dump me," I responded as I walked her direction.

"Sure looked to me like it," she raised her eyebrows as if in wait for an explanation.

"I don't believe it's fair to her if I discuss the conversation's intricacies with you, so I'll hit he highlights. We went to dinner. She had hopes it would turn into a more in depth relationship. I, on the other hand, had no intention of pursuing anything romantic with her. She explained her hopes. I explained, or at least attempted to explain, my lack of desire," I smiled, satisfied at having explained the situation delicately.

"Wow. You make it sound like a business transaction," she said as she placed her hands on her waist.

"Not at all. Or at least it's not my intent. She was sweet, just not what I desire in a mate. There was no value in continuing. It would not have been fair to her or to her emotions," I explained as I motioned to the empty chairs.

"Listening to you talk is like reading a textbook," she said as she turned toward the table where she was previously seated.

"I'll sit for a while, let me grab my stuff," she said as she rotated her wrist and looked down at her watch.

In returning with her purse and magazines, she sat down and smiled. Her hair appeared to be more light brown than blonde. With her right side facing the storefront windows, her hair shimmered in the sunlight. Satisfied to be seated with her, but feeling somewhat like a modern day pimp, I crossed my arms in front of my chest.

"I'm not going to attack you, don't get defensive already," she said as she pointed to my chest.

"Excuse me?" I responded, with one eyebrow slowly rising.

"Your arms. They're crossed. It's a defensive posture. Anyway, I don't have much time. I just thought we could talk. I won't bring up the girl or talk any more shit. Promise," she said as she extended her hand over the top of the table.

"Okay," I smiled, pleased at her gesture.

I took her hand in mine and shook it, finding the surface of her palm surprisingly rough. Although I preferred holding it to not, I quickly released it from my grasp so as to not make her feel self-conscious regarding her leathery skin. As I began to consider the cause of her rough skin, she smiled and placed her hands in her lap.

"So, I've been coming here for years. And in the last week or so, I have seen you here twice. Never previously, but twice in the last week. What gives, Parker? It's Parker, right?" she asked softly.

"Yes, I'm Parker. You've got a good memory," I hesitated; somewhat frustrated that she wasn't sure of my name.

"I just graduated college and after becoming employed, moved to the neighborhood. I live here in Old Town. I just found this place a week or so ago, and I like it. It's a nice place to relax. What's your fascination with it?" I asked.

"I come here to read. Dream. Relax. Find bits and pieces of myself I'm afraid I may not find elsewhere. Generally, before work," she raised her right hand from her lap and brushed her hair behind her ear.

"What do you mean? Bits and pieces of yourself?" I asked, intrigued by her statement.

"You know. Well, *you* probably don't. I work as a prep cook in El Cajon. I take care of my mother when I am not working. The two consume me. So, the three places one might find me? Here. Work. Or home. That's it. I come here to read my books, magazines, and dream," using her right hand, she turned her head slightly and raked her hair behind her left ear.

"You don't do anything else?" I asked.

"Nope."

"Ever?" I asked.

"Never."

"Out to eat? Go to a bar? Hit the beach?" I asked.

"Nope. Nope. Nope."

"I'm sorry you aren't able to get out more. And regarding your mother, if I may ask, is she sick?" I asked softly.

"I guess you could say that. She was injured years ago. She suffers from chronic incurable pain. She's addicted to painkillers, and for the most part, bed ridden," she responded, raising her left hand from her lap and clenching her fist in her palm.

"I see. Sorry to hear that. Your dreams are?" I asked, my voice trailing off, inviting her to respond .

"To be a chef. To live a normal life. To have a family. Not a husband and kids kind of family, but a father, mother, brother, and sisters. I guess that's about it," she responded, rubbing her palms together.

"No siblings? You have no brothers or sisters?"

"I have a mother. That's it," she said as she stood from her chair.

"I'd love to stay and talk, I really would. I like talking to you for some reason. But I have to get to work, I'm sorry," she placed her purse strap over her shoulder and began to gather her magazines.

"I'll put them away. Go ahead. Thanks for taking time to talk," I smiled and nodded my head slightly as I stood.

"I'll get them," she responded.

"I insist," I chuckled.

"Fine," she shook her head and turned toward the steps.

I watched as she began to walk down the steps, filled with gratitude to have seen her again. As she began to gracefully walk away, I recalled Kenton's remark, which I was now asking myself several times a day.

If this were my last day on this earth, would I do anything different?

"Victoria," I shouted, quickly making my way to the staircase.

Halfway down the steps, she turned to face me.

"Yes?"

"Your number. I would like to get your number," I placed my hands on my hip and raised my eyebrows in wait.

She stopped, sighed, and stared at me for a long moment.

"I don't know why I'm doing this. Fine. Six one nine four four seven one zero three five," she smiled.

I smiled in return and repeated the number silently until she walked through the front door.

I walked back to the table and began to pick up the magazines she had left. As I straightened them, making note of what she was reading, I noticed a scrap piece of paper that marked one of the pages. As I removed it, I saw something had been written in pen on the other side. Curious, I turned the piece of paper over.

One word, neatly written in block lettering.

My first name.

Parker.

PARKER

Growing up, for me, wasn't necessarily difficult. Accepting life as it unraveled into my lap, on the other hand, was a different story. My grandmother proved to be instrumental in my ability to understand most things regarding living life.

"Life is hard. No, life is tough," I complained as I walked into the kitchen.

I may have been eleven or twelve at the time. Frustrated from what had been, in my opinion, a difficult day at school – I had expressed my opinion regarding life and its hardships to my grandmother.

"Parker, life is just that. Life. Living it is easy. It happens while we're alive, without thought or effort. Even if or when we choose to do nothing, the clock continues to tick. From our feeble beginning, through all of the complications, and to what will certainly be an unscheduled and unwelcome ending, life *happens*. Life is easy. Live it while you're alive."

"Because when you're gone, Parker, you won't have an opportunity."

I wouldn't have necessarily described my grandmother as an intelligent woman, but I always admired her for being wise. She seemed to have a different outlook on life, and her outlook, for the most part, became mine as time passed.

"What about mom and dad? Why did they have to leave here so soon?" I asked as I placed my books on the table.

"I suppose it was to bring us closer together," she smiled, opening her arms to hug me.

Slowly and sadly, I walked to her and wrapped my arms around her waist. Her dresses always felt smooth against my skin. I pressed my face against her shoulder and took a slow deep breath.

"And grandpappy?" I asked as my eyes began to fill with tears.

"Again, to bring us even closer," she responded as she pressed her hands against my back.

"Things happen in life, Parker. Things we may or may not understand, at least not at first. These events, these happenings, they provide us with opportunities. It's God's way of opening doors for us. He provides us with opportunities, and we must make choices. If we're of sound mind and practicing being a good child of God, we'll generally make good choices," she placed her hands on my shoulders and slowly broke our embrace.

"Your parents leaving this earth gave your grandfather and me an opportunity to do what we believed to be right, to raise you no differently than we raised your father. We took that opportunity. And you, Parker, are the reward. You're a fine boy. There's none finer, if you ask me. Not now or ever," she looked down into my eyes, her hands still resting on my shoulders.

"Life is easy. All we have to do to live it is breathe. Making all the right choices regarding life and living it takes some serious thought, though. Try asking yourself this before you make a decision regarding living your life, Parker," she paused and widened her eyes.

"If I had to tell my grandmother about this, would I still do it? If the answer is yes, it's probably a good decision. If the answer is no, I wouldn't suggest doing it," she smiled and turned toward the kitchen counter.

She removed a platter of cookies from the countertop and placed them on the table beside my books.

"Now, let's sit and have a cookie. Tell me why life is so difficult today," she smiled as she removed a cookie from the platter and bit it in two.

I pulled the chair away from the table and sat down. As I reached for a cookie, I began to explain my frustration.

"It's Jessica. She has a boyfriend," I sighed.

"The little blonde girl in your class?" she asked.

I nodded, still angry about my discovery of Jessica having a boyfriend.

"And how does this change your day from good to bad?" she tilted her head to the side and waited for my response.

"I liked her," I said sadly.

"Did you ever express your fondness to her?" she asked as she reached for another cookie.

I shook my head.

"So, you liked this little girl, but you never told her so?" she asked as she dabbed the crumbs from the corner of her mouth.

"No ma'am," I looked down at my feet as I responded, knowing one of life's lessons was headed my way.

"Well, let me see," she wiped her mouth again and smiled.

"When something in life happens that we take exception to, something we don't like or wish would have gone differently, we need to take a step backward," she paused and reached across the table lifting my chin with her index finger.

"And ask ourselves if we had an opportunity to do it all over again, if there is something we would have done differently. So, Parker, knowing now what you know about your feelings for this girl, and your frustrations about her having a boyfriend, would you have done anything differently?" she looked down into my eyes and waited for me to respond.

Embarrassed, I shrugged my shoulders.

"Parker..?" she said slowly, dragging my name along for a good five seconds.

"I suppose I would have told her how I felt," I responded.

"The good lord gave you an opportunity, Parker. You chose not to take it. And now? Well now he is teaching you a lesson. Learn it. And move on through life a wiser soul. The next time Parker, the next time do things differently."

"Yes ma'am," I responded.

My grandmother may not have always been right, but the advice she provided me always made sense at the time she offered it. From the time I was in kindergarten, she spoke to me as if I were an adult. My speech patterns, vocabulary, and manner of expressing myself vocally were either a result of her teachings or my constant absorption of literary works from her library. At an early age she challenged me to read and read often. After a few years, the challenge was unnecessary – I could never read enough to satisfy my desire.

I suspect reading was an avenue of escape for me as a child – a means of becoming a character in the book for a short period of time. If a story was well written, I would often read it multiple times, inevitably enjoying the latter readings fractionally more than the first. I found myself more drawn to fact based fiction and less to the world of fantasy. Fantasy was difficult for me to digest; primarily because I was certain it could or would never happen.

The year before I graduated from high school Jessica and I became intimate. Proudly, we announced our relationship to everyone who cared to listen. I walked the hallways of the school hand in hand with her, pleased to call her my girlfriend. One thing led to another, and not unlike any other seventeen year old high school kids in a relationship, we considered having sex.

I didn't express my sexual desires to my grandmother, but I didn't have to. One evening, while eating dinner, she began a conversation about life. Initially, I wasn't uncomfortable, but as always with my grandmother, where the conversation began and where it ended were two totally different subjects. She had a very effective manner of introducing a topic she wished to discuss.

"If you were able to turn back the clock and change one thing about your life, any *one* thing, what do you think you'd chose, Parker?" she asked as she pierced another piece of pot roast with her fork.

As she began to chew her food and wait for my response, I thought about her question. The first thing that came to mind was to live a life with my mother and father. Reluctant to blurt out my initial thought, I considered my answer, making certain there was nothing else I wanted to say.

"I would want to have my mother and father in my life," I responded.

"I imagined that'd be your response. And why do you imagine you chose *that* for your answer?" she asked between bites.

I scrunched my brow. Her reasoning behind asking such a question wasn't quite clear to me. As always with my grandmother, she formulated her questions to elicit thought. I lowered my fork to my plate and considered what life would be like with my parents in it. After a long moment, I responded.

"So we could be together – a family; mother, father, and son. I like it here, and you're like a mother to me, but," I paused, trying to thoughtfully decide what it was I wanted to say.

"You don't need to say any more, Parker. I understand. Every parentless child wants to have what so many take for granted; to have a conventional family. It's quite natural. Now, let me ask you another question," she placed her fork onto the edge of her plate and cupped her hands together.

"Have you and Jessica discussed having sex?" she raised both eyebrows slightly and inhaled a shallow breath.

If I had food in my mouth at the time, I am quite sure I would have spit it out. The question, even from my outspoken grandmother, shocked me. Uneasy and somewhat uncomfortable answering, I began to shift my weight in the seat of my chair.

I crossed my legs.

I crossed my arms.

But I knew I had no other choice other than responding truthfully. My grandmother had one rule regarding responding to her questions; *always respond truthfully*. She advised me from a very early age to always tell the truth. If I told her a lie, there would be hell to pay. If I told her the truth, regardless of what it may be, we could always figure out a way to get through it. Considering all things, I kept my response truthful and quite brief.

"Yes."

"Well," she paused and glanced toward the china cabinet.

"I want you to consider a few things. Regardless of the birth control used, none are one hundred percent effective. So, there's always a chance of pregnancy being the result of a sexual encounter. Considering the chance exists, ask yourself this, Parker. For a little bit of pleasure, are you willing to take the risk of Jessica becoming pregnant? Because if you're not able to spend the remaining days of your life with Jessica raising your child, there will be another son or daughter in this world feeling the way you feel right now about your parents. Alone and without," she looked down and into my eyes as she spoke.

I continued to squirm in my chair uncomfortably and listen to what she had to say. At that particular moment it wasn't what I was hoping to hear, so sitting still and listening intently wasn't high on my list of current priorities.

"So, if you're not ready to become a parent – if you're not certain that she's *the one*, my recommendation would be to wait – because there's always that one chance. And after it happens, undoing it isn't really an option. So Parker," she paused in mid-sentence as I fidgeted in my chair.

As she sat and waited for me to make eye contact with her, I stopped squirming.

"My recommendation is to only have sex with a woman if you're comfortable she's the woman you'll be with forever. If you truly believe in your heart of hearts you can happily be with her forever, and you're comfortable she feels the same about you, go right ahead. If not, think about that child growing up without a family. That's the only advice I have about sex, Parker. Now eat your roast before it gets cold," she said as she picked her fork from her plate.

Jessica and I didn't last much longer. The thought of her becoming pregnant and my becoming an irresponsible and incapable teen father filled me. Ultimately, I knew I was in charge of my sexual advancements, but nonetheless, the thought of screaming infants and irresponsible parents became common. My relationship with Jessica was short lived, and to date remains my only relationship with any female with a love interest. I lived in constant fear of a child being brought up in a single parent home – the product of two irresponsible teens.

As I grew older, the same types of thoughts prevented me from being in any form of meaningful relationship with a woman. I had countless *friendships* with women, but sooner or later they always wanted more. For me, *more* meant a screaming infant and a failed relationship – a risk I wasn't willing to take.

As an adult, we stand as an extension of the beliefs, principles, and moral fiber of those who played an active participant in our upbringing. I'll be forever grateful for my grandmother being who she was, and believing in what she believed in with such vigor. Her beliefs, over time, became mine.

I miss her more than she'll ever know.

PARKER

"Mr. Ward is out for the morning. How is your day, Mr. Bale?" Downes asked as I walked toward the steps.

I paused in mid-stride, frustrated at the fact that Kenton was gone. I hadn't slept much the previous night, and was already quite frustrated. Kenton's absence wasn't helping matters much. I really felt a desire to talk to someone.

Downes stood on the edge of the steps in black linen pants and a short sleeved linen shirt. The shirt was a silvery-blue color, and although it fit loosely, it didn't come close to disguising his rather muscular physique. I stood, wondering if he intended for people to be intimidated by him.

"So far, great. Thank you," I fibbed.

"So, if I may, is your first or last name Downes?" I asked as I slowly approached the base of the steps.

"Let's walk to the back deck, Mr. Bale. We can talk over a glass of tea. Please," he motioned toward the front door as he spoke.

I followed up the steps, down the corridor of the home, and through the French doors onto the deck. Downes, as always, walked quietly, and methodically. He seemed to be the type of person that spoke only if necessary, and probably never for the sake of speaking alone. As he sat at the table where Katelyn and Kenton and I sat only a few nights before, I realized a pitcher of tea and two glasses were already positioned on the table.

"It's raspberry, and I must say it rivals the peach. Oh, and for what it's worth, your eyebrows are repairing nicely. The other night it appeared you had four of them," he hesitated as he held the pitcher suspended over the table.

I nodded my head and smiled as I brushed my index fingers along my brow. As he poured me a glass of tea, he grinned. His teeth were perfectly shaped and defined the color white. *Probably veneers.* No one has teeth quite that perfect.

"Sometimes I get carried away plucking them. I'm surprised you noticed," I sighed as I lowered my hands nervously to my lap.

"I notice everything. It's my job," he grinned and inhaled a short breath.

"My mother's maiden name was Downes. She chose to name me Downes, using her maiden name for my first name. So, Downes Tallert was born," he said, continuing to smile the entire time.

"I see. It's an unusual first name, I like it. And your last name. It's unusual as well, but it sounds familiar, I just can't seem to place it," I said as I raised the tea glass to my lips.

"I've grown to like my first name. I never much cared for it as a kid, but it's perfect for me as an adult. So, how's the search coming along?" he asked.

"Excuse me?" I responded.

The question didn't make much sense when he asked it. After I responded, I realized he was probably asking about my quest for women. Feeling fractionally uneasy regarding the situation with Katelyn, I rolled my eyes.

"Alright I suppose," I said as I wiped the condensation from my glass of tea.

"It's certainly an interesting job description. Mr. Ward spent countless hours drafting the contract. It's interesting at minimum," he said as he lifted his glass.

It dawned on me as he spoke that I had never actually took time to read the entire contract. At the attorney's office, I had merely signed the agreement based on Kenton's statement of the conditions of the contract, I had not read it. Eventually, after taking a copy home, I flipped through it, but didn't read it.

"You'll probably think I'm crazy, but I've never actually read it," I chuckled.

"Oh really? I assisted Mr. Ward in drafting it, so I'm quite intimate with the contents. It's a simple contract, but you should read it; you're bound to the conditions of it, you know," he pushed himself away from the table and slumped slightly into his chair.

"I suppose I will read it eventually. Right now it doesn't really seem to matter," I continued to slide my finger along the glass and wipe the beads of condensation from the surface as I spoke.

"Is something troubling you, Mr. Bale?"

Surprised that he asked, I wondered if there were telltale signs which caused him to ask the question. Although there was nothing I could pin point, I had both began the day and continued through the morning feeling somewhat *off*. Not knowing why or what caused me to feel the way I was feeling, I wanted to talk to Kenton.

For whatever reason, Kenton provided me with a level of comfort I wasn't able to attain elsewhere. Maybe his absence was making me even more uneasy and Downes could sense it. I looked up from my water droplet fascination and focused on the horizon.

"I'm not sure, but I just woke up feeling strange," I responded as I stared over the putting green and out at the ocean.

"Physically ill, or mentally off balance?" Downes asked as he crossed his legs.

Although I had never been to a psychologist or psychiatrist, I felt as if Downes was acting the part. His voice, as always, was quite soft and monotone. There was a certain comfort I felt from his presence as well. His physical presence, military-esque haircut, and the fact that Kenton revealed his activity in the war, however, made me somewhat hesitant to warm up to him.

"Mentally, I suppose," I responded as I realized condensation had once again formed on my glass.

"I see. What's changed in the last few days?" he asked as he raised his hands to his chest and rubbed his palms together.

As he rubbed his palms together, his forearms flexed. I watched as his muscles flared from just above his wrist to the exposed lower portion of his bicep. Although I had never really given it much thought, it was possible Kenton had chosen Downes as his assistant for many reasons, a body guard being one of them.

"Not too much, I don't guess. I told Katelyn I wasn't interested in proceeding. She didn't take it well, called me a douche," I grinned, wiping my curved finger along the edge of the glass.

"You surely hadn't developed an attraction to Katelyn yet, so would I doubt you're feeling uneasy because of that alone. Have you had any reflections or thoughts of your past that might be troubling you?" he asked.

What would cause him to immediately ask such a question, I thought. More than likely he was correct, but who would jump to such a conclusion so promptly? In thinking of how to respond, and what just might be the cause of my uneasy feelings, I stared at the base of my glass of tea.

"Considering *my* past, it was always easy for me to dwell on certain thoughts, events, or ideas, and become a product of my second guessing myself. I believe, at least for me, becoming comfortable with the fact that I couldn't change my past left me with no other option but to embrace the fact that I was left to accept it for being just what it was," he paused and leaned into the table.

"My past. And I sure can't change it," he smiled and shook his head slightly.

"Do you have things you regret or wish you could change?" I asked as I looked up from my glass of tea.

"I suppose my knee-jerk response should be *yes*, but it's not going to be my answer. There are probably a good handful of people that would look at my past and say I had quite a bit to be either ashamed of or without a doubt regret," he paused and began to shake his head again slowly.

"I have no regrets. To regret my past would be to admit I am not satisfied with who or what I have become. Everything I have accomplished and all I have been exposed to – good or evil – has created what sits before you. If I look solely at the reflection I make today, I stand proud. So in short, no Parker, I don't have things I regret," he grinned softly as if satisfied with his response.

"I'm sure sometimes I think of events of my past and feel sorry for myself. Not something I do often, but it does happen. Overall, I think I'm happy with who I am and what I have accomplished so far. I'm self-driven to succeed, I guess that's a good thing," I said as I looked down at my glass of tea again, realizing my response wasn't nearly as uplifting or full of emotion as Downes'.

"I imagine it would be difficult to come to terms with losing both parents at such a young age. Feeling sorry for one's self would probably be quite common," he said softly and almost apologetically.

"It's something I think about more often than you think," I responded, still staring at my glass of tea.

"Wait a minute. How did you know?" as I asked, I realized Katelyn may have told Kenton during my half hour of subconscious Katelyn-less bliss.

"Mr. Ward's background investigation of your past revealed it," he responded.

"Background investigation?" I sat up in my chair and became a little more focused.

"You didn't think Mr. Ward would have offered you such a position without knowing anything regarding who you are, did you? And, it's public knowledge – anyone can find out. You realize that, don't you?" he stated in a matter-of-fact tone.

I felt proud and ashamed at the same moment. Part of me felt proud that Kenton had performed a background investigation on me, and still had interest in me working for him. I had nothing to hide, and I am quite proud of everything I have accomplished. Additionally, I felt ashamed I didn't realize this was something he had done. It was a surprise, and I now felt foolish.

"I guess I never really thought about it. It's probably common for an employer employee relationship like this one, I suppose. To do a background investigation, that is," I became a little more comfortable as I spoke, realizing it wasn't anything grotesquely uncommon for an employer to do.

Downes leaned forward again, resting his massive forearms into the edge of the table, "I would say in a situation such as this one, it would be mandatory. At any rate, were your parents a portion of what you were dwelling on in the last few days?"

"Yes sir. I suppose so. That and recollections of my grandmother's wisdom. It's depressing thinking about being alone. You know, without family," I said sadly.

"Your grandmother passed as well, if I remember correctly," he said, raising his eyebrows slightly.

I didn't like admitting it, but she was gone. She had passed the summer of my junior year of college – of breast cancer. Something she had fought for years and didn't bring to my attention. I didn't like being reminded of it, and in fact, preferred denying she was gone. I looked up and did the only thing I felt I could without losing my composure.

I nodded my head.

"Well, for what it's worth, you can always look at Mr. Ward and me as being family. Now and always," he said, turning his palms upward and smiling as he finished speaking.

"Thank you. But one day this will all end. This job won't last forever," as I responded I began to feel a little more hollow and alone.

"Quite the contrary. Mr. Ward doesn't nor has he ever allowed a friend to slip from his grasp. In fact, he has very few people he considers friends. I would venture to say you, me, and Mr. Astur would satisfy the list entirely," he nodded his head slowly as a form of reassurance.

"Really?" I sat up in my chair, astonished at what he had said.

"Do you really think he considers me a friend?" I asked.

"Mr. Bale, I don't *think* he does, I know so," he responded.

"But. Well, he hasn't known me for long. It just seems like he'd be more inclined to get to know who I was and in time," I paused and raised my index finger to my lips.

"In time he would develop a friendship with me. Or. Well, I don't know," I began to feel satisfied Downes statement was an accurate one.

"Mr. Bale, Mr. Ward selected you from a large group of people. The factors which played the largest part in his decision making were *who you are*. You're an impressive individual, Mr. Bale. Very much so," he reached for the pitcher of tea and poured himself another glass.

"If I remember correctly, there were twelve applicants. It was an exciting meeting for sure," I grinned, recollecting Kenton's intimidating demeanor during the meeting.

"Mr. Bale," Downes shook his head as if in disbelief, "at that juncture, there was only one applicant. *Only one.*"

I sat and stared, trying to decide what it was Downes was trying to say. To the best of my ability, I attempted to recall the conditions of our first meeting. Was it possible Kenton investigated me prior to my having met him? Had he made the decision to hire me before we had even met?

Highly unlikely, I decided.

The advertisement was posted the morning of our first meeting. I responded to the ad, and was called in for an interview. During the meeting, Kenton tossed the contract in front of me and asked if I was a risk taker. I signed the contract, and he gave me keys to a car. There was no way he could have even known I existed before the morning of the meeting. Clearly, I was tired, and my mind was attempting to work overtime.

"What did you mean by the comment? There was only one applicant?" I asked, hoping Downes would continue.

He shook his head slowly from side to side.

"I have offered too much as it is. Just know this, Mr. Bale. Mr. Ward admires you," he said as he turned to face the ocean.

"Admires me?" I blurted excitedly.

Still staring out at the ocean, Downes nodded his head once sharply.

The thought of Kenton admiring me was almost laughable. I certainly admired him. His brutal honesty was difficult to dismiss and without a doubt almost impossible not to admire – at least not for me. In fact, I aspired to one day become Kenton Ward, or at minimum as close as I could muster.

"So, have you met anyone new?" Downes asked.

"Well, kind of. We'll see what happens. I may bring her here to meet Kenton if things go well between us. I'm still somewhat embarrassed about how things went with Katelyn. I suppose I'll wait and see how things go with this one," I responded.

The thought of Victoria made me smile slightly.

"Well, if you're going to take her out on an actual date, you really don't have a choice. Eventually, Kenton *has* to meet her," he turned from facing the ocean and looked at me as if confused.

"What do you mean, I don't have a choice?" I asked, puzzled at his statement.

"Mr. Bale, I recommend you read the contract. Entirely," he responded.

Based on that particular statement and a few which preceded it, I knew there was one thing I needed to do, and do very well.

I needed to read the contract.

VICTORIA

"As soon as you're done with the onions, peel the tomatoes, they're ready. We need to have everything for the bisque done this afternoon, we're serving it tonight," Tony stood in front of me, his hands on his hips as he shook his head.

"I know we're short staffed, but I can get it done, don't worry," I responded, my eyes fixed on the onions scattered over the prep table.

"Stop talking and start chopping," he said as he turned and walked out of the kitchen.

Angelina's is the only kitchen I have ever worked in, and I would like to think other restaurants have a more understanding staff to work with. Here, almost every weekend, someone doesn't make it to work. Typically, it was Tony's nephew. I never miss a day of work, so inevitably I work harder, later, and under more scrutiny than most of the kitchen employees here.

I find it frustrating, but there isn't a lot I can do to change it. More than anything I want to open my own restaurant, and someday witness people enjoying the foods that I design, prepare, and serve. Today, this is nothing short of a dream. Today, I must do what I am asked, and do it without arguing or complaining. Today I need my job, my paycheck, and the experience.

"I'll have everything done in an hour, Tony. Don't worry," I smiled as I looked up from the onion I held in my left hand.

"Stop fucking talking and start fucking chopping. I'll be back in thirty minutes. You better be done Vicky," he said as he turned and walked away.

'Yes sir," I responded.

I hated being called Vicky. Tony was the only person who ever did it with any regularity. He said it was too difficult to say Victoria, and Vicky took less time and effort. To me, calling me Vicky was no different than calling me Lisa. It wasn't my name.

In addition to daydreaming about having my own restaurant, I often dreamed of walking into the kitchen and telling Tony to go fuck his self. Maybe tossing a handful of onions across the kitchen, kicking one of the half a dozen plastic buckets that littered the floor, and screaming a few choice words on my way out.

The fact of the matter was that I would work at *Angelina's* as long as they would employ me, and do whatever they asked of me. Ten dollars an hour wasn't much money for someone my age, but it was all I could expect to earn at an entry level position in a kitchen. Working my way up the ladder *here* was probably nothing more than a dream. For now I needed the dream to provide me with the devotion and dedication to continue.

For now, I needed the income. Without it I would be incapable of taking care of my mother. For now, I am all that she has. I suppose she is all that I have as well. We need each other, and I need this job. As I began to peel the tomatoes, I thought of Parker and his fabulous smile.

The way he dressed.

How he smelled.

He seemed so down to earth. To find someone as charming and attractive as he was and have that person possess one ounce of humility was almost impossible, at least in southern California. Being humble wasn't on a list of character traits that most men attempted to achieve in San Diego. Being an arrogant asshole was. Parker seemed well grounded and intelligent. Parker seemed like the type of man who would stay in a relationship and remain devoted to his woman.

As I scooped the tomatoes across the prep table and into the stainless steel pot, I smiled. The thought of Parker was fulfilling, and although he was beyond what I could describe as attractive in both appearance and stature, eventually he would do what all men do.

He would leave.

"You get done with those tomatoes?" Tony barked as he walked into the kitchen.

"Yes sir," I responded, "I just finished."

He turned his wrist and looked down at his watch. Slowly, he turned and walked toward the metal rack on the wall that held our timecards. After removing my time card from the rack, he studied it for a moment, and turned to face me.

"Paulie is on his way in. Go ahead and get out of here. We'll get it from here," he said as he slid my timecard into the time clock and pressed the button.

"I was really hoping for some overtime. I'm willing to stay all day."

"You're hoping for it, and I'm not willing to pay it. I'd suggest getting gone, you're off the clock, Vicky," he said as he dropped my timecard into the empty slot.

"Yes sir."

As I walked to my car, I heard a faint sound from my purse. Although the noise wasn't a familiar one for me, I certainly recognized it. My phone beeped, indicating a text message had been received. A typical twenty-three year old probably received a hundred text messages a day. I, on the other hand, haven't received a hundred text messages in my entire life. There weren't half a dozen people who had my phone number, and of those who did have it, one of them may have the ability to text me.

One.

Parker Bale.

I leaned against the car and removed my purse from my bag. Pressing on the *text message* icon revealed several text messages from an unfamiliar number. Excitedly, I pressed the screen with my thumb, opening the first message.

Victoria, this is Parker. There was once a girl in my life I was fond of, and I didn't tell her until it was too late. Before I developed enough courage to speak, she had a boyfriend. Disgusted, I sat through my classes in high school and

The length of the message was such that it was separated into several small messages. Excited to continue, I fumbled to press the next message and continue.

was forced to watch as she and her new boyfriend flirted and walked the hallways hand in hand. I told myself the next time I was fond of a girl, I would tell her promptly. I realize you're busy with work and your mother, but I would be

Again, the message ended. Smiling from ear to ear, I pressed the screen, revealing the next message.

grateful if you could find the time to meet me for another cup of coffee or something similar. With a warm heart and a cheesy grin, I can assure you of one thing. Victoria, I am fond of you.

I stood and stared at my phone. *Victoria, I am fond of you.* I could feel my heart beating in my throat. Without much thought, I pressed my thumb into the reply window of the open message, and typed a response.

How about now?

I pressed send.

I scrolled to the first message and began reading from the beginning again. Something about listening to Parker speak was satisfying, and this message was no exception. After reading through the message entirely twice, I dropped my phone into my purse, smiled, and opened the car door.

Standing with the car door open, I turned and looked through the parking lot. I don't really know what I was expecting to see, but the lot was as I would have imagined it to be at noon on a Saturday.

Empty.

I lowered myself into the seat and fumbled with the keys. As I attempted to get the keys into the ignition, it became apparent just how excited I was. I looked down and watched the key shook in my hand. As I rolled my eyes and thought again of the message, my phone beeped.

Like a hormone filled teen exposed to her first case of puppy love, I snatched my phone from my purse and swiped the screen with my thumb. From the same number, I had received another message. Above all of the others, and unread, it wasn't necessary for me to open the message to read it. Both typed words the new text message contained were visible on the screen. I grinned and pressed the message anyway.

Splendid. Where?

After glancing at my watch, I realized it was time for lunch. Additionally, although I had planned on working all day and night, Tony had just relieved me of my duties for the day, leaving my schedule open. My mother sitting at home with a fresh bottle of OxyContin eliminated the need for my immediate return. In most senses, I was free for the day; a rare occurrence indeed.

Caught up in the thrill of the entire text messaging event, I typed a response before I had time to really think about it. Generally speaking, I wouldn't go with a man anywhere, especially with one that expressed an emotional attachment to me. My life, my lifestyle, and my lack of faith in the male species prevented me from really ever doing anything with a man. Nonetheless, I pressed *send* without thinking. I looked down at the message I had sent and waited.

Want to grab a bite to eat?

Instantly, the phone beeped. I pressed the unread message, opening it, and looked at the screen.

I'll meet you at Antonelli's Deli on Magnolia in fifteen minutes. Sound good?

Fifteen minutes in Saturday's traffic was entirely possible. I pressed the clutch pedal to the floor and turned the ignition. With a little luck and a slight nervous bite into my lower lip, the car started. As the engine warmed up, I typed a message to Parker.

Yes.

I pressed *send*, and grinned at the thought of meeting Parker for lunch. Holding the clutch to the floor, I pushed the gear shifter forward. As usual, the gears made a grinding sound as I pressed the shifter into gear. With self-taught precision, I pressed the gas pedal to the floor and released the clutch, sending the car lurching forward.

I needed to try to get there before he did. I really didn't want him to see what I was driving. It was embarrassing enough for me to look at; I couldn't fathom someone else actually *seeing* it. As I weaved my way through traffic, my mouth watered at the thought of Antonelli's Veggie Sub.

And seeing Parker.

PARKER

I don't suppose I will ever really know if my elevated level of excitement was a result of meeting a woman in general, specifically meeting Victoria, or in part because of a feeling most people typically mistake as love and later attribute to *fate*. I did, however, know one thing for sure.

The sandwich I was eating wasn't helping matters.

"Holy crap," the words escaped before I had a chance to think about what I was saying and where I was.

Victoria looked across the table and grinned as she shook her head. Holding her veggie sub firmly in her hands, she opened wide and forced two more inches of the overstuffed sub into her mouth.

"I'm sorry, but this sandwich is beyond fabulous," I apologized after I swallowed the bite I was chewing.

"I'm not even going to try to be tactful," she said through a mouthful of sandwich she attempted to chew, holding the remaining portion of her sub at arm's length and nodding her head.

"If you can't accept me for who I am, just leave when you're done eating, because there's no sense in continuing," she paused and swallowed what remained in her mouth as she studied the six inches of sandwich left behind.

"Watch this. I'm going to devour this mother fucker," she growled as she successfully shoved half of the sandwich she was holding into her mouth.

Seeing Victoria have the comfort to act like herself was reassuring. All too often I'm left wondering if the person or persons that I encounter, spend time with, or befriend are actually behaving in a manner that they would if they were alone. Generally, I convince myself that at least a portion of the person's personality or behavior is in fact a facade, or some form of feeble attempt to impress me.

She was certainly impressing me, and all she was doing was eating a sandwich as if I weren't present. As I became lost in another bite of Antonelli's ham, salami, mortadella and provolone sub, Victoria looked over the table, her eyes widened in a cartoon like manner. With her mouth held open by the inch of sub sandwich that from extended past her lips, she attempted to speak.

"Duh," she mumbled as she clapped her palms together and raised her hands above her head.

"Pardon me?" I asked, not even coming close to understanding what she had attempted to say.

Leaving her left hand extended above her head, she lowered her right hand even with her face and pulled all but one finger into her palm, leaving her first finger pointed upward. Slowly, she pointed her index finger at the end of the sandwich which remained exposed, and pushed it into her mouth. After a few exaggerated chews, she spoke again.

"*Done*. I said I was done," she grinned as she finished chewing.

"Oh. I see that. Did you enjoy it?" I asked as wiped my mouth with my napkin.

"Mmmhhhmmm," she groaned.

"This is one fantastic sandwich, as far as sandwiches go," I admitted as I looked at the three inches of remaining sandwich.

"Are you always proper, or do you loosen up at all? You know, as time passes," she asked.

I placed the sandwich onto the paper wrapper it was served in, and raised my hands to my face in wonder. No differently than I had admired Victoria for being herself as we sat eating, I too was acting and being myself. Nothing added or taken away from the way I would always act. Not having spent much time as an adult in the presence of women, I wondered what she must think of me. She was interested enough in me to meet me for lunch, but I didn't want her to lose any of her interest.

I had no intention of attempting to become someone or something I was not, either. I wanted Victoria, or anyone for that matter, to fully accept me for who I was, and not for what they wished me to become. After careful consideration, I looked at Victoria intently.

"The person seated before you is truly me. I'm predictable, I suppose. I am always proper, or at least pretty close," I responded as I reached for the remaining portion of my sandwich.

"Shove it in your mouth, all of it," she laughed.

"Excuse me?" I asked as I lowered my sandwich.

"The sandwich. Shove it in your mouth. All that's left," she grinned.

"Why would I want to do that?" I asked.

"Because it's fun?" she responded as she cocked her head slightly to the side.

I raised the sandwich to my mouth and studied it. Without a doubt, I could inhale what still lingered in one bite. To prove to myself I could physically do it, and to ensure I could also act in a manner other than what was proper – at least for a moment – I shoved the entire sandwich into my mouth. What followed took a matter of seconds, but will remain with me for a lifetime.

As I chewed the sandwich, or at least attempted to do so, some of the lettuce became separated from what was in my mouth, and fell into my throat. The small shredded pieces of lettuce tickled my throat, causing me to cough. The fact that I didn't care to spit my sandwich out onto the table combined with the fact that at least generally I attempt to act in a gentlemanly manner caused me to close my mouth tighter.

A combination of my forcing my lips closed and inhaling what was a required amount of oxygen to keep me alive naturally forced what little loose lettuce that remained into my already sensitive throat. That small amount of lettuce caused me to cough again, forcing another natural inhale, and the subsequent choking.

Upon inhaling, some meat matter became lodged in my throat. Although multiple times as a child I *claimed* to be choking, and I have seen many people make the same claim, I now *knew* what it felt like to choke to death. Attempts to cough and or breathe became completely unsuccessful. I was not able to do anything which required the use of my lungs. As I waived my arms frantically, my eyesight became blurred. Hearing, after a few short seconds, became quite difficult and eventually faded to being total deaf. Total blindness soon followed. At some point in time during the process, I must have stood, because I now felt my weakened oxygen starved knees give way to the earth's gravitational pull. As I felt myself collapse onto the floor, I was certain I would die on my first date with Victoria. A mouth full of sandwich and a piece of salami lodged in my throat, the paramedics would announce my death upon arrival.

Parker Bale. Dead at twenty-three, a victim of being a stupid sandwich eating fool.

After an amount of time I had no means of measuring, I felt my body being lifted to the heavens. Although blind and deaf, I could feel myself slowly and steadily being raised from the floor. Thoughts of Victoria left me as visions of finally being with my parents and grandmother filled my mind. Suddenly, I felt a sharp pain in my chest.

The fatal blow.

A heart attack.

Simultaneously, I coughed, spit the contents of my mouth onto the table, and regained my vision and hearing. And then, the chest pain hit me again. I looked down. Two small hands, one clenched into a fist, pressed sharply into my chest. I looked up and across the table. Although my vision remained blurred, I could see Victoria was gone. I coughed again. As my eyes watered and I gasped for another breath, I looked over my shoulder. Despite my being embarrassed, I felt compelled to thank my savior.

And the angel of life who stood behind me – her arms wrapped tightly around my midriff – was the same angel of death who coerced me to attempt to eat an entire sandwich in one bite.

Because it would be fun.

Victoria.

VICTORIA

Life's greatest treasures will never be held, purchased, or bartered for. They will only be felt.

Having the ability to feel is the greatest gift God has ever given.

Parker causes me to feel.

When we feel a particular way, we may not like it or agree with it, but the feeling exists within us regardless. Changing how or what we *think* is a relatively easy task. I compare changing how we *feel*, however, to lighting a fire and placing our hand in it, then and convincing our self it doesn't burn. It's impossible. I don't have a tremendous amount of experience socially, and although I don't *know* this to be true, it's possible Parker and I actually connect with each other on many different levels. When I am with him, I feel courageous and inquisitive. These aren't feelings I am necessarily comfortable with, but I feel them nonetheless. In the presence of men in the past, I felt skeptical and distrustful. With Parker, I find myself saying and doing things so far beyond what I would *normally* be comfortable with, but oddly enough I *am* comfortable.

It felt as if I was blossoming.

Parker and I have had experiences and exposures in life which mirror one another. Considering this one aspect of him alone, it would stand to reason he would understand how and why I feel a particular way more accurately than any other person who doesn't have the experience or exposure he has.

As time passes he'll eventually become who he truly is. If it so happens and he is who he *appears* to be, I could spend a lifetime enjoying our time together. If he eventually materializes as a different person, and his true self emerges in contrast to what I believe him to be, I'll be forced to make a decision. For now, my decision is to give him the benefit of the doubt. Based on how he makes me feel, I'd be a fool to do otherwise.

And a fool I am not.

"It's like magic. Magical. Whatever. I love it," I slowed my pace of walking slightly and inhaled deeply.

"I think part of it is the smell," Parker said, his arm trailing behind him with my hand still in his.

"I agree. I have always loved the smell. It's soothing. Sometimes a really shitty day for me is turned into a peaceful night if I get a whiff before I go to bed," I smiled and took a long step to attempt to catch up to him.

The smell of the beach was peaceful to me. It was almost as if it cleansed me as I breathed it in. Although I lived in a coastal city, it was not always easy for me to find the time to make it to the beach. I've often wished I could just plop a home down in the sand and stay there forever, going to sleep and waking with the scent and the sounds it brings. As we walked along the edge of where the ocean meets the sand, I pressed my toes into the sand with each step, leaving my best impression of our existence.

My mark.

Victoria's beach, stay away.

As he lightly held my hand in his, he turned and smiled. I looked down at his pants, which were cuffed to mid-calf. He looked cute. Knowing his dress shoes were in trunk of his car – because they wouldn't fit in his blazer pocket – made him just a little bit cuter. He didn't need much help in the looks department. His facial expression was generally one of someone in the middle of a business negotiation, but he was beyond handsome. His brown hair was always perfectly cut, as if it were trimmed daily. He kept it short on the sides, close to the length of the Marines stationed along the coast. The top was long enough to fall into his face if he'd allow it to.

But he didn't.

His eyes were brown, but not brown like mine. My eyes are *primarily* brown, but have little flakes of green in them. Parker's eyes were brown as if someone had painted them with brown paint. I hated to stare at them, but something about them was the same as Parker himself – different.

"Personally, I enjoy the *sound*. You know, when there's not a tremendous amount of people here. When it's quiet. The sound of the waves against the beach, it's almost hypnotic," he lightly squeezed my hand as he spoke.

I turned toward him and smiled without speaking. Walking along the beach on a summer night while holding the hand of a member of the opposite sex wasn't on my list of to-do's when the summer started, but now it was a reality. I must admit I could get used to this without much effort.

On the east coast, facing the horizon and staring out into the ocean, the sun rises from the ocean every morning. On the west coast it sets into the water at night. I've never decided which would be best to witness, but for now at least I was stuck with the sunsets.

Parker and I had walked along the beach for a mile or so, turned around, and were walking back toward where we began. Together, we were able to witness the sunset along the beach, and now it was slowly getting dark.

"I could get lost in watching your face express your moods. Your face changes as you walk, think, and probably smell the things you enjoy," Parker said softly.

I tilted my head and considered making a smart-assed comment, but chose to smile instead. Pushing him away would be natural for me, but I wanted to enjoy this as long as I could. As I stood and smiled, I realized we had stopped walking. I glanced to my left and noticed we had walked back to where we started – our cars parked in the parking area above the edge of the beach was a reminder that this night was over.

It was time for me to go back to the reality of my house filled with the noise of a blaring television and my narcotics induced semi-comatose mother.

"I like looking at your face, too," I breathed, "you're pretty."

"Pretty?" he asked.

I turned and looked behind me, hoping to see the impressions we had left in the sand – proof of our existence along the beach – confirmation this night had actually happened just as I believed it did. The beach was void of our footprints. The waves had washed them all away, leaving nothing but smooth sand where we had walked. The only hint we had been here would be the memory I would carry with me and the impression we were leaving now.

"Yes, pretty," I responded as I twisted my feet into the wet sand.

"Thank you," he said as he smiled and tugged my hand lightly; reminding me our time together was in fact coming to an end. I wanted to resist, allowing the night to go on forever. As we walked up the beach I pressed my feet into the sand firmly, leaving an impression deep enough to last a lifetime.

And I did not look back.

PARKER

I've never had expectation of doing anything with my life but obtaining the current goal I have placed in front of me. Eventually, I always set another objective and proceed with a new venture. I have consistently set realistic targets, achieved them, and moved on to my newest aspirations. My life invariably has advanced one goal at a time. Striving to obtain them gives me reason to live life.

I have often wondered what – if any – satisfaction is obtained by a person who has few or no goals in life, and proceeds through the course of a day by purely existing. Allowing life to merely *happen* and accepting whatever may land in your lap has never made a tremendous amount of sense to me.

My life so far has been a series of small pieces which will eventually come together to make larger pieces. I have always assumed the large pieces, over time, would assemble to make a whole. A completed puzzle. The puzzle of life solved one small piece at a time.

Victoria and I had been seeing each other for short periods of time as they became available to her for almost a month. I cherished the time we spent together, and had come to look forward to it more than I would have ever guessed. It was as if I *needed* to see her to feel accomplished. In her absence, my only concern was when would be our next available opportunity to meet. All of our time together had been a result of us *meeting*, and not necessarily a *date*. The fact that we had not been on an actual date *yet* allowed me to justify not having introduced her to Kenton.

It was as if I felt a need to shelter her from him and him from her. In my mind, to allow her to meet Kenton would be confirmation she was in fact the product of some type of experiment, some test, some game I had played, and she the poor pawn. In my eyes, at least right now, she was not a part of my employment or *the contract* in any way, shape or form.

Sitting outside on two benches opposite each other, we had been eating frozen yogurt and talking. Today, as time passed, I became more and more satisfied simply sitting, feeling the sun's warmth against my body, and witnessing Victoria do – without effort – what she did best.

Satisfy me.

"For the first time in my life, I am not concerned with an *achievement*," I scooped the small plastic spoon around the edge of the container, hoping for one more taste of the Vanilla frozen yogurt.

"Explain," Victoria muttered as she spooned another huge wad of yogurt into her mouth.

"Well, I have lived my life by setting and achieving one little goal at a time, and that goal was my only focus until it was completed. Unless I could check it off the list, I had nothing else I focused on. I've always had a target in front of me, and it's my *only* focus. Right now, I don't necessarily have one, and I don't care," I shrugged.

I tipped the cardboard container to my mouth and tapped my fingers against the bottom. It was without a doubt empty. Frustrated, I placed it on the bench beside me and inspected my fingers for residue.

"We all set goals. It's natural. Want some of mine?" she asked as she extended her hand toward my face, the small plastic spoon overloaded with coconut covered yogurt.

I grinned and opened my mouth. Victoria was a different type of person than I had ever been exposed to. Not that I necessarily led a sheltered life, but I had never been much of a social butterfly either. As she spooned the yogurt into my mouth, she giggled. Seeing her smile was far more satisfying to me than I would have ever imagined. It was if I had some vested interest in her happiness. Seeing her smile and sharing something as simple as frozen yogurt with her actually provided me with a form of satisfaction unlike any other.

"It's just that," I paused and contemplated my thoughts as I swallowed the yogurt.

"Well, I don't know that I can even come close to describing it," I hesitated and looked down at her shoes.

"I grew up with my grandmother as my best friend. Everything I needed was obtained through her. Every ounce of praise, pat of reassurance, and feeling of satisfaction I received was a result of my exposure to her. I didn't receive nor did I ever *attempt* to receive it through others. I completed high school, and went on to attend and graduate from college. My completed education was my goal. I obtained it. My next goal was employment. I achieved that one as well. Now, although employed, I don't necessarily have a goal, short or long term. Oddly enough, I don't know that I want one. Now, right now, it's as if something changed in me. I'm happy just being. Simply *existing* satisfies me as long as you're part of the existing," as the words escaped my mouth, I felt as if someone else was speaking through me.

I looked up and opened my arms as if embracing the entire outdoor seating area. The thoughts and feelings I possessed were new to me, and I had not yet spoken with anyone regarding how I felt. Simply stating my thoughts and what I was feeling caused me to come to believe my life may be changing before my very eyes.

"Wow. Huh. Interesting," she paused and raised the plastic spoon to her lips and bit against it.

"Well, you've always lived a structured life and now you feel like you can let loose and become whoever it is that you're supposed to become. I think we're all who we are at birth, and it's just a matter of time before we emerge our true selves. Sometimes it takes longer for it to happen. Maybe, for some of us, it takes an event or some happening to open our eyes to who we truly are. Oh shit. *Oh shit,*" her voice elevated as she pressed her hands against her thighs.

"The fuckin' salami. It was the when you choked on the salami sandwich," she shouted and stood from the bench.

"What?" I stood up as she rose from her seat.

"Last month, when you choked on the sandwich and I saved you," she laughed, "it was some form of spiritual awakening."

A spiritual awakening, as Kenton had described. He had described the event in the restaurant with Downes and the mother of the fatherless child as a spiritual awakening. By his own admission, it changed him from being a self-centered asshole into who he is today. Victoria could be right – perhaps it was the salami incident and my almost dying from choking on the sandwich. Maybe it was enough of a scare that it caused me to take a step back and look at my life's accomplishments as nothing more than life itself. Quite possibly I have lived my life void of any resemblance of true emotion. Or, the presence of Victoria in my life caused me to realize I needed someone more than I had previously thought.

Maybe the path of our life *is* predestined at birth, as Victoria believes, and I'm simply finding myself. I suppose I could be determining who and what it is that I am to finally become. In a sense, I'm finding myself.

"Maybe you're right. Maybe it was the salami, I don't know," I hesitated, looked down at my shoes, and attempted to mentally formulate the remainder of my response.

I truly felt confused.

"It was," she said solemnly.

I considered what I wished to say, and shook my head to clear my thoughts. After a brief moment, I attempted once again to speak my mind.

"I'm not sure identifying *what* got me to this point is even important. Recognizing the changes in me, embracing them, and allowing – or I guess *accepting* them is what's important. Earlier I kind of fumbled around with what I really was trying to say. Ultimately, what I wanted to say was that I love spending time with you. Sharing things with you makes me smile. So thank you. And let's not stop this anytime soon," as I looked up and into her eyes she smiled.

"I think we're both seeing changes in ourselves. I know I have. I've always hated the thought of spending time with a man. Men suck. They're all after one thing and one thing only. After they get it, they move on to trying it with someone else. I haven't got time for their bullshit. And then along came you. Dressed in your little dress shoes, with your perfectly manicured nails – yeah, I noticed," she paused and pointed toward my hands.

"And your blazer over your designer tee shirt. You interested me Parker," she turned and tossed her empty yogurt container in the trash.

"But there's so much more to you, Parker Bale, so much more. The more I get to know you, the more I grow to love who you are. So far, there's really nothing wrong with you that I can see. You're polite, kind, and you always say the right things. Sometimes you're rather wordy with your explanations, but I think I have your grandmother to thank for that, and it's part of what makes *you* you. And, what else did you say?" she slowly raised one eyebrow and stared into my eyes.

"*Let's not stop this anytime soon?* Yeah, right. You're never going to get rid of me. Never. Because *this?*" she waved her hand in a circle as she pointed down toward the sidewalk.

"This is only the beginning," she smiled.

VICTORIA

I had come to cherish my time with Parker more than I ever dreamed possible. I now not only yearned to spend time with him, I felt it was necessary to survive. I didn't like feeling as if I *needed* someone – in fact, it left me rather uncomfortable. I don't think I'll soon share my feelings with Parker, because my emotions and desires may be advancing far more rapidly than his.

For now, I'll sit and hope this never changes.

His absence causes me to question his existence as well as his devotion or interest. I often feel I should send him a simple text message just to have him respond – anything to prove he is still somewhat interested in me. Everything he does indicates his interest in me is consistent, but for some reason I want *proof*. I have a difficult time believing he'll maintain this level of enthusiasm considering my position on premarital sex. He claims to possess the same moral standard I do regarding sex, but I find it difficult to actually believe him. For now, I don't *want* to believe him, I *must* believe him. It allows me to hold onto this feeling that fills me every night as I lay in bed. I have fallen in love with Parker Bale.

And I am scared to death.

"It's green, you dumb bitch, go already!" I screamed out the window of the car.

Either my screaming or the fact she finally emerged from the fog she was living in caused her to look up, realize the light was green, and accelerate. I pressed the clutch pedal, shifted my car into first, and mashed the gas pedal to the floor. As I carefully released the clutch, the car began to lurch forward.

And the light turned red.

Fuck.

I pressed the clutch and allowed the car to roll back into place behind the intersection. *I'm going to be late.* I squeezed the steering wheel in my hand and turned my wrist. A quick glance at my watch revealed ten minutes time before I was to meet Parker for lunch. I only had to go two more blocks, but for some reason I was having a difficult time.

It was one of *those* days.

As the cross street's light turned yellow, I depressed the clutch and shifted into first gear. After a heavy foot on the accelerator, I was ready for this light to turn. I sat anxiously in wait until…

Green.

My tires screeched as I lurched forward and into the intersection. Fuck yeah. I shifted into second gear without letting up off of the gas pedal, released the shifter, and flipped my hair over my shoulder. Confidently and quickly, I glanced in the rear view mirror. As I shifted into third gear, I squinted and moved closer to the mirror. It almost looked like…

Great, I'm covered in sweat.

For some reason, since I started seeing Parker, I began to sweat. Either that or I began to notice *I sweat*. Regardless, in the last month or so, I've been sweating profusely. Without any activity or reason, I look like a gym rat or a professional athlete – one who has just finished a competition. As I attempted to blot my brow with the palm of my hand, I noticed the light at the intersection in front of me turn yellow.

And red.

I pressed the gas and accelerated through the light. A few honking horns reminded me it wasn't the best of ideas, but it was over now. I pressed the clutch pedal to quiet the engine and turned into the alley which led to the parking in the rear of the restaurant – where the employees park.

Parker wouldn't see my car if I parked it here.

Parker always parked in the street so he could keep an eye on his car, and for good reason. He had a very nice car and he needed to keep it that way. Mine, on the other hand…I dreamed someone would steal it. No one, however, dared. Hell, maybe several have tried for all I know, and weren't able to keep the engine running. One advantage of owning a piece of shit car is that no one *wants* to steal it. In my particular case, no one was probably *able* to steal it.

I stepped out of the car and slammed the door. I turned to face the car, my key firm in my hand, and began to lock the door. As I started to turn the key in the lock, I laughed to myself and hesitated. Without locking the door, I pulled the key from the door lock, unzipped my clutch, and dropped my key inside then zipped it closed. Still smiling, I peered around the corner of the back of the building into the alley toward the street.

Clear.

I took a shallow breath and walked briskly toward the street. At least for now, I had no desire to have Parker find out what I drove or where I lived. Introducing him to my mother was not an option. Not that she'd have a problem with it. Hell, she'd love him. But *I* had a problem with it. Her condition was embarrassing. I truly believe she remains in pain of some sort, but not as much as she continues to claim. And certainly not at a level which requires the degree of sedation she remains in. For now, I'll have just a few secrets.

As I approached the restaurant entrance, I heard a shout from across the street. Parker, as always, stood outside his car waiting. He motioned for me to come to him, which I found a little odd. His being parked across the street and nowhere near an intersection would require me to jaywalk – or walk to the intersection and use the crosswalk. I looked toward the traffic light. *Two hundred yards.* I looked at Parker.

And ran.

"*Stupid bitch!*" a motorist screamed as he honked his horn and flew past me.

He was close enough my dress blew against my legs. I stopped in the center of the street and allowed the cars to zip by me as I waited for another break in traffic. As soon as I saw an opening, I sprinted for the other side.

And Parker.

With his mouth open and his eyes widened, Parker caught me in his arms as soon as I hopped onto the curb beside his car.

"That was exciting," I gasped.

"I can't believe you did that. There's a crosswalk right over there," Parker said as he nodded his head toward the intersection a hundred yards away.

"Yeah," I took a deep breath and smiled, "but I wanted you to catch me."

He shook his head and scowled, "Had I known you were going to do that, I would have brought it to the restaurant."

"It?" I asked.

"Well, I got you something. I wanted to give it to you. I've been standing here waiting, but I didn't see you drive up. Where did you park?" he asked as he released me from his arms and stepped toward the car.

Got me something?

I tilted my head toward the restaurant, "Other side of the street, duh."

Got me something?

He shook his head as he pulled an envelope from the car. Smiling, he stepped in front of me as he held an envelope close to his chest. Standing in front of me grinning, he looked like a little boy. A very handsome little boy. A very handsome little boy clutching an envelope.

Got me something?

I pointed toward the envelope, "Is that for me?"

He nodded his head once sharply.

"Let's wait until we get into the restaurant," he said.

I turned and pointed toward the street full of cars, "So, why'd I run across the street?

He grinned, "So I could catch you?"

"Okay, now I'm dating a comedian. Hand it over, please," I said as I help my hand out and smiled.

He placed the envelope in my hand and smiled.

Carefully, I unsealed the flap with my fingernail. As I pulled the card from the envelope, I couldn't help but smile. I had hoped it was a card, but as Parker held it I couldn't tell. As a little girl, probably until I was around seven or so, my mother always gave me birthday cards. After that, as she became more disoriented and sedated, she stopped getting me cards – and telling me happy birthday for that matter. No one else, at least that I can recall, has ever given me a card of any type.

The outside of the card was simple. Three beautiful flowers as if they were painted with water colors. And what appeared to be hand written, but was part of the printed card, the words *just wanted to let you know*.

Eagerly, I opened the card. Only hand written words were inside. I looked up from the envelope and smiled at Parker, and quickly looked back down to read the card.

Victoria,

I cherish the time we spend together. Sometimes I believe I have such deeply seated feelings I expect those around me understand how I feel. That, of course, is not always the case. For that simple reason alone, I want to take time to tell you...

You mean the world to me.

And I want to do whatever I must to keep you beside me.

So please, and I am begging you...

If I ever do anything wrong, and I hope I never do, please take time to tell me.

Because losing you would surely be the death of me.

Yours,
Parker.

I swallowed a lump in my throat. I reread the card entirely. I attempted unsuccessfully to swallow again. I reread the card. As I attempted to refrain from crying, I looked up.

Parker's hands were pressed deeply into the pockets of his slacks. His perfectly pressed white shirt had the first button unbuttoned and his Blazer fit his broad shoulders perfectly. How could I not love this man?

"Did you like it?" he asked softly.

I clutched the card in my right hand and raised both my arms above my head. Slowly, Parker's face filled with wonder.

I closed my eyes, "No. I *loved* it. Kiss me."

"Right here? Out in the open?" he asked.

I nodded my head and waited.

As I felt his body press against mine, I lowered my hands around his back, careful not to bend my card. His hands pressed into my lower back, pulling me into him softly. As his lips met mine, and we began to kiss, my entire body turned to goose bumps.

And Parker Bale kissed me for the first time.

VICTORIA

Contributing something meaningful into a conversation hasn't always been easy for me. Generally speaking, what I offer isn't received in the manner it was originally intended, so I tend to listen more than I speak. With Parker, I had never felt as if anything was misinterpreted. I generally understood what he had to say, and if not I was never afraid to ask for an explanation. As far as I could recall, he had never taken exception to anything I had said either. For the most part, we communicate well with each other.

As I have never really had the opportunity or necessity to communicate with anyone but my mother, I didn't have a tremendous amount of experience doing so. It's highly likely my lack of communication skills made speaking with others, and doing so accurately, quite difficult. Considering how Parker and I seemed to naturally understand each other allowed me to look at this one aspect of our relationship as being very valuable.

"How can you *not* believe in them? They're for real," Paulie hissed.

"There's no such fucking thing as aliens, dude. Jesus," Vincent shook his head in disbelief.

"The fuck," halfway across the kitchen floor, Paulie stopped and stared at Vincent.

"Dude. Seriously? You think there's spaceships and shit flying around? Really?" Vincent rolled his eyes and continued to chop the celery.

"I *know* there is. If you don't think so, it just shows how fucking stupid *you* are," Paulie said as he spit into the trash can.

Paulie hadn't done anything all morning. He always seemed to find a way to spend all of his time doing nothing, and actually worked harder to make sure he wasn't doing what was expected of him. Typically, Vincent and I picked up the slack. As frustrating as it was, there wasn't much I could do or say about it. As I listened to the two of them argue, I continued to cut up the chicken we were going to use in the wild rice soup listed on this evening's menu.

"Dude, you know if Tony sees that, he's gonna be pissed. He said to stop that shit," Vincent hesitated and waited for Paulie to respond.

"Fuck Tony, he's my pops brother. It's not like he's gonna actually *do* something about me chewing tobacco," Paulie snapped, "and just so you know, *he* believes in aliens."

Paulie paused as he walked toward the sink and turned to face Vincent.

"All I'm saying is if you think that life just stops here on earth, you're one shallow assed dude. If it can live *here*, it can live in other places. C'mon, Vinny," Paulie whined.

"Dude. There's no oxygen or anything on other planets. And nothing to eat or anything. No food. And there ain't any fucking gravity either," Vincent shook his head and began chopping the celery again.

"Victoria? What do you think?" Paulie turned to face me and waited for a response.

I didn't care for participating in discussions with Paulie and Vincent. There was never a simple conversation between them. It was always an argument, and generally it began with Paulie trying to force his belief down his friend Vincent's throat. I continued cutting the chicken, and responded without looking up.

"I don't know that I truly believe one way or another, Paulie. I'm open-minded. I wouldn't be surprised either way," I said flatly.

"See? Victoria believes in them," Paulie shouted, pointing my direction.

"That's not what she said, dude. Give up. Tony's gonna be..."

Vincent didn't finish his sentence when Tony stormed into the kitchen.

"What the fuck are you dip-shits doing? I said the soup had to be done before lunch. How the fuck am I going to serve that shit this afternoon if it isn't done before fucking lunch?" he stood in the threshold of the door with his hands on his hips.

"Betsie what's her fuck is coming in here tonight. I told you we *had* to have this shit ready. How the fuck is she going to review the restaurant if there's no fuckin' soup? I fucking *told* you," Tony growled.

Clearly, he had a conversation with Paulie earlier and Vincent and I weren't part of it.

"They were arguing about dumb shit, uncle Tony. I told them we were behind. I told 'em that chic was coming to review the restaurant. They've been dicking off all morning," Paulie complained.

The hair on the back of my neck rose as Paulie stood in front of Tony and lied about having spoken to Vincent and I. Staring down at the knife I held, I continued to quietly work and wait for this to end. Eventually, Tony would walk out angry, and we'd continue to make progress against the dinner deadline.

"So what's so fucking important you'd rather be jacking your gob than working, Vicky?" Tony turned and asked.

Desperately, I wanted to explain to Tony what a complete piece of shit his nephew was. I wanted to tell him he spit tobacco in the trash can again. I wanted to convey how Paulie believed in spaceships and thought aliens were going to abduct people on some predetermined day in the month of May next year. Truth be known, Tony probably believed it too. As my jaw tightened, I looked up from my work and glanced around the kitchen.

"Nothing, Tony. Just trying to finish with the chicken," I smiled.

"Oh really? So, you callin' Paulie a liar?" Tony asked.

"No sir," I breathed.

"So you *were* dicking around all morning instead of working?" he walked through the doorway and into the kitchen as he spoke.

"No sir," I responded.

"So Paulie's lying?" he asked.

I pursed my lips and clenched the knife in my hand. Slowly, I drew a breath through my nose and exhaled before I began to speak.

"I…" as I attempted to speak, Tony interrupted me.

"Are you *angry*, Vicky?" Tony began to mock me as he walked my direction.

"Watch out uncle Tony, she got a knife," Paulie laughed.

I hate confrontation. I simply hate it. All I wanted to do was come to work, do what was asked of me, and eventually be promoted into a position I deserved. Having a superior who was capable of recognizing my strengths and weaknesses, and be willing to help me when I didn't understand shouldn't be too much to ask for. Instead, I had this kitchen full of simple-minded Italian testosterone.

I looked down at the plastic bucket of chicken skin beside my feet and drew another short breath.

"I asked you a fucking question, *Vicky*," Tony said as he slapped his hands down onto the edge of my prep table.

We don't *always* plan what happens in our life. Sometimes, things just unravel. Later, I suppose we may look back on the event or happening and wonder if we should have done something different. Either way, once it's done, it's done. Undoing it is never an option.

"Fuck you," I shouted as I dropped the knife onto the prep table.

"Fuck you and your worthless assed lazy fucking nephew. I wasn't arguing," I raised my right foot behind me as if I were going to kick a field goal for the San Diego Chargers football team.

As Tony looked down at my foot, I swung my leg forward and kicked the bucket of chicken skin across the kitchen floor. As the bucket bounced off the wall behind Tony, bits and pieces of chicken exploded into the room. I reached behind my back and began untying my apron.

"Go fuck yourself, Tony. You don't appreciate shit. I worked hard for you, and you never appreciated it. Not once. And my name isn't Vicky, *asshole*," I shouted as I tossed my apron on the floor in front of him.

"It's Vic-tor-i-a."

And, just like that, my employment with *Angelina's* ended. I never quite understood who *Angelina* was, but I imagine whoever she was, she wouldn't appreciate Tony treating people the way he did.

And I bet Tony never called her *Angie,* either.

Fucking asshole.

PARKER

Nervously, I had explained matters to Kenton regarding Victoria. I suspected he knew I was doing *something*, but he had been patient with my not presenting someone to him. His expectations of my measurable advancements were potentially far different than what I believed they were. Either way, he listened intently as I explained about Victoria and my feelings for her. Feeling somewhat guilty, I made clear our plans to go on a date, and my understanding of my obligation to introduce her to him.

Although I had not taken the time to read the contract entirely, I had spent a little time skimming through it. Promptly, I found the portion Downes referred to regarding Kenton's requirement to meet the women I chose to take on a date. After reading that particular section, I once again tossed the contract aside, feeling no real need to bore myself with the incidental remaining contract language.

As the date to meet Kenton approached, I began to feel odd about introducing her to him. I struggled with the idea of her being someone I was contractually bound to see, and our time together not being by my choice. I finally settled with the idea of her being nothing more than what she was, and Kenton being nothing more than what he was. A woman of true interest to me, and a man who found value in witnessing me treat her in a gentlemanly manner.

When I thought about it in this particular fashion, it didn't seem awkward at all. So, with my view on matters somewhat askew, when the day arrived, we made our way to Kenton's mansion. Now, sitting in the same room where Kenton and I had once shared our first sandwich, I listened as he talked to Victoria.

"Just like that?" Kenton chuckled.

"Just like *that*," Victoria snapped her fingers.

"Called him a *motherfucker*, just like the piccolo player," Kenton began to laugh.

"The what?" she laughed.

"Oh, it's an old joke, I'll tell you in a minute," Kenton sighed.

"I called him an *asshole*, I think. I really don't remember. But definitely not a motherfucker. At least I don't think so," she grinned.

"Well, either way. Good for you. Having a boss that doesn't appreciate you isn't very rewarding. And Parker," Kenton paused and turned to face me, "remind me to never call Victoria by anything other than her given name."

"I'll remind you," I grinned.

"So," Kenton stood from his position in the chair.

"One Sunday morning, down south at a southern Baptist church, the choir began to sing. Although the congregation didn't realize it initially, they soon found out there was a new piccolo player playing along with the organ as the choir sang. He was nothing short of awful," Kenton paused and smiled as he alternated glances at Victoria and I.

"So, after a few torturous songs, someone in the crowd hollered, *the piccolo player's a motherfucker.*"

"The reverend of the church stood up, shocked that someone would say something so awful, especially during the service. *Who called my piccolo player a motherfucker?* He hollered out into the congregation."

"No one responded."

"Frustrated, the reverend pressed his hands into his hips. *Alright, if no one has the courage to speak up, I want the man sitting next to the man who called my piccolo player a motherfucker to stand up*, the reverend said."

"And, no one stood up."

"*Alright,* the reverend said, *I want the man who's sitting next to the man who sat next to the man who called my piccolo player a motherfucker to stand up.*"

"And again, no one stood up."

"Aggravated to no end, the reverend stepped to the front of the pews and looked over the congregation, *I want the man who's sitting next to the man who's sitting next to the man who sat by the man who called my piccolo player a motherfucker to stand up.* He stood, furious with anger and waited. The church sat silent."

"After a few long seconds of silence, a man seated in the rear of the pews quietly stood.

"*Reveren', he said.*"

"*I ain't the man who was sittin' next to the man who called the piccolo player a motherfucker. I ain't that man, reveren'. And I ain't the man sittin' next to the man who sat next to the man who called the piccolo player a motherfucker. And I ain't the man who called the piccolo player a motherfucker, either. Reveren', I ain't none a those things. But reveren' what I got to know is this,*" Kenton paused, raised his eyebrows, and inhaled.

"*Who called that motherfucker a piccolo player?*"

Kenton laughed so deeply upon telling the punchline he fought to catch his breath. Almost immediately his laughing became so hard his eyes were watering. As he continued to cough and slap his knee with one hand, he raised his free hand to wipe the tears from his face. Having never seen him act like this, I began to laugh as well. I turned to face Victoria, who began laughing.

"*I want the man sittin' next to the man who was sittin' next to the man…*" Victoria laughed.

"Oh hell. I'm sorry, Parker. I had to tell it. I've always loved that joke," Kenton wiped his eyes and sat down in his chair.

"I enjoyed it," I chuckled.

As we all sat attempted to catch our breath, Downes stepped into the edge of the room from the kitchen hallway.

"Mr. Ward?" he motioned into the corridor as he spoke.

"Excuse me," Kenton said as he stood from his chair.

Slowly, he walked into the hallway with Downes.

"That Downes makes me nervous. He's big and scary. Is he Kenton's bodyguard or something?" Victoria asked in a shallow whisper.

"Actually, he's quite nice once you get to know him. Really. And no, he's just Kenton's friend. He's like an assistant. Maybe he's kind of like a filter between Kenton and the normal day-to-day bullshit someone like him is exposed to. He pays the bills, and greets guests. I don't know. But he's actually nice," I said softly.

Almost immediately, Kenton walked into the room and sat down into his chair. With a tone of disappointment in his voice, he sat on the outer edge of the cushion and spoke.

"Well, I'm sorry to say this, but Karen has fallen rather ill. She won't be cooking dinner for us like I had hoped. I actually didn't realize so much time had passed. We've been sitting here talking for almost four hours. Maybe we can all get in my SUV and go get something to eat," he sighed.

"Or I could drive," I said.

"What was she going to prepare?" Victoria asked softly as she stood from the loveseat we were seated on.

"Excuse me?" Kenton asked.

"What was she going to cook? What does she have available?" she asked.

"Oh, I'm not sure she got that far along, why?" Kenton responded.

"What's wrong, Victoria?" I asked as I stood.

"Oh, nothing's *wrong*. I was just wondering. I could cook for us. I mean, if you'd let me, sir," Victoria said.

"*Let* you?" Kenton chuckled.

"Karen shows up here every day no differently than she would to a normal job. Her sole purpose here is to prepare meals. I pay her for her services. I can't expect you to..." in mid-sentence, Victoria interrupted.

"I know you don't *expect* me to. But I *want* to. Please," she whined.

"Very well," Kenton smiled as he stood.

"Downes," Kenton shouted.

All but instantly, Downes opened the door and stepped into the room.

"Yes?" Downes asked into the open room.

"Show Miss Fisker into the kitchen, please." Kenton said.

"Very well. Miss Fisker, follow me." Downes said as he turned toward the doorway.

"Victoria. Please, call me Victoria," she smiled.

"You better do what she says, Downes. She just might kick a bucket of chicken guts your direction and call you a motherfucker," Kenton chuckled.

"Very well, Mr. Ward," Downes nodded his head once toward Kenton.

"Victoria," Downes continued as he motioned to the doorway.

Naturally, I began walking in Victoria's direction as she followed Downes out of the room.

"Stay here and visit. It won't take long, and I won't need any help from either of you two. Sit down, both of you," Victoria demanded.

Not knowing what to do, I turned to face Kenton. As he lowered himself into his chair, he motioned toward the loveseat.

"Sit," he said, shaking his head from side to side.

"She's a piece of work, Parker. I must say, I'm quite attached to her already. She's got a fabulous personality. And she just," he paused and rubbed his forehead with his index finger as he looked down at the floor.

"She fits," he said as he looked up.

"She fits," he said again, nodding his head slowly.

"Just what does she fit?" I asked.

Kenton leaned forward in his chair and rested his elbows on his thighs. As he lowered his chin into his hands, he smiled.

"She fits *you*. We all have strengths and weaknesses, every one of us. Naturally, our lives *need* balance. Yin and Yang. They're concepts used by the Chinese to describe how opposite forces are actually complimentary of and to each other."

"I know, the little symbol," I said as I drew a circle in the air with my index finger and made an "s" shape through the center.

"Chinese philosophers are of the belief, and I must say I totally agree," he paused and outstretched his arms, curling both his palms upward.

"Light and dark, up and down, hot and cold, fire and water, and life and death for that matter are all physical manifestations of yin and yang. These opposites literally require each other to form a component in which the whole is greater than the assembled parts. She's the yin to your yang, son," he sat back in his chair and nodded his head.

"No differently than the teeter-totter you played on as a kid. When you stood up, the thing would drop your friend to the ground like a stone. It required both of you sitting on it to be balanced. It doesn't mean for two people to succeed they must be polar opposites, it's much deeper than that," he sighed and scrunched his brow slightly.

"I understand," I said as I nodded my head.

"Do you?" he asked, looking up and in my direction.

"I think so. I don't know what it is about her, but she makes me feel *different*. I know that. *Why* she does it isn't as important as the fact that she does. You and I both know I don't have a ton of experience in dating women and such, but I can say she certainly makes me feel like the search is over. I don't want to look for anything or anyone else, Kenton. It's difficult for me to think of tomorrow coming and not having her included in it."

Simply saying what was on my mind caused me to realize the feelings I had developed for Victoria were not only real, but seated very deeply. I sat on the edge of the loveseat full of gratitude I had someone like Kenton to speak to about what I was feeling. Although he was much younger than my grandmother, I imagined he would be about the same age as my father, if he were still alive. In some ways, I was beginning to look at Kenton as a fatherly figure. He was filling a void left in my life by the untimely departure of my grandmother. And so far, he was doing it all too well.

"Tell her how you feel, and include her in all of your tomorrows, Parker. If you're able, that is. She fits you," he stood from his chair and began to step toward me.

Naturally, I stood from my seat as he stood. As I did, he extended his hand in my direction. Confused, I reached for his hand. As he took my hand in his and shook it, he smiled a smile of tremendous pride.

"Parker, I'm proud to call you a friend. You're one of few I can say this to. In a short period of time I've come to really care for you, son. I really have," he said as he shook my hand.

"Likewise," I nodded.

As I spoke, I got a feeling in my throat as if I wasn't going to be able to continue to speak if I tried. Emotion seemed to fill me as I stood with his hand in mine. Having Kenton treat me in the manner he did wasn't something I expected when I agreed to be in his employ. He truly acted as if he cared about me. His advice to me was heartfelt and well thought out. He had yet to offer me shallow meaningless advice, for which I was grateful. His statement of being friends and calling me *son*, however, was a little more than I expected. I realized he didn't intend for me to receive the *son* remark in the manner in which I did, but for now it filled me with an unfamiliar warmth – warmth I am now certain I have yearned for a lifetime to feel.

As I released his hand, I noticed Downes walking into the room.

"Miss Victoria is ready, gentlemen," he said with a tone of authority.

"Victoria, Damnit. I heard that. I'm not *Miss* anything. I'm Victoria, you big goof," I heard her scream from the kitchen.

Downes widened his eyes and smiled as he turned around and began to walk through the doorway. Kenton and I stood simultaneously and started walking in his direction. As we followed him into the kitchen, I watched as Victoria placed the fourth plate onto the table.

"Hurry, before it gets cold. Pan sautéed filet mignon with caramel-brandy mushroom sauce, what appeared to be some fairly fresh green beans, and garlic mashed potatoes. I threw the salad together with vinaigrette, so no choice on dressing, fellas. Come on, let's get to it," she said as she pulled a chair away from the table and stood beside it.

"Sit down, you big fucking brute," she motioned toward Downes as she spoke.

Downes chuckled and turned toward Kenton as if waiting for approval to sit.

"Sit down, Downes. This is *her* show," Kenton laughed as he walked around the table, looking down at the food placed carefully on the plates before him.

"You know," Kenton said as he sat at the bench beside Downes.

"I bought this table at Downes' recommendation. I really liked the look of it," he paused and traced his hand along the top of the table.

"But I don't think I've sat down here for one meal yet," he turned toward Victoria and smiled.

The table was very large and rectangular in shape. The top was constructed of an oiled butcher block approximately four inches thick. The outer legs were held together by a rustic steel rod with a turnbuckle in the center. On one side was a leather covered wooden bench, and on the other, large wooden chairs with leather seats. It was very fitting for the stainless steel and wooden theme of Kenton's kitchen.

"Well, although I love to cook, and I've memorized about every recipe I've ever read, this is the first time I've actually cooked a meal for a group of people. My mother doesn't really eat, so I primarily cook for myself. So, if it helps, this concept is new for both of us. Come on, let's eat," she said as she sat down beside me.

"It's almost as if we're a family," I said as I looked across the table toward Kenton.

As I spoke, Victoria reached over and squeezed my hand lightly in hers. I realized as she held my hand she probably felt the same way I did. Her living a life of solitude with her sick mother prevented her from being able to enjoy the things most people take for granted. A straightforward meal with friends to her and I was something much more.

"I hate to muddy the waters, but if I sit at the table to eat, I have to say a simple prayer. It's a requirement of sorts, I guess. It's been a long time since I've done anything like this, so I'll make it brief," Kenton said as he looked down at his plate and clasped his hands together.

I squeezed Victoria's hand lightly in mine as I closed my eyes.

"Lord. Please bless this food we are about to partake of so it may strengthen and nourish our bodies, allowing us to serve you further. I thank you, Lord for placing these people in my life, people who are far more than friends, Lord. Lord, we sit before you tonight and ask that you bless this food as a family, one which I am truly grateful you've blessed me with. And we ask these things in your name, Amen."

I opened my eyes.

A family.

Although I was touched deeply by Kenton's rather poignant prayer, I became concerned Victoria may view what he said about being *a family* as somewhat pretentious. My entire body filled with emotion, I turned to face her, hoping for some form of assurance she was comfortable with everything Kenton said. As I did, she rotated to her left, leaned into me, and rested her face on my shoulder. As she turned her head to look up into my eyes, she smiled.

"I think I'm falling in love with you, Parker. Now eat, before it gets cold," she whispered.

Incapable of speaking, I simply stared and smiled.

These opposites literally require each other to form a component in which the whole is greater than the assembled parts.

She truly was the yin to my yang.

PARKER

Kenton paused and leaned onto the shaft of his putter, "I don't make promises I can't keep, and I'll never say something I don't truly mean. So, I will rarely provide assurance to anyone about anything. Inevitably something goes to hell in a hand basket and it later makes me out to be a liar. But let me tell you something Parker Bale. And I can assure you of this."

Nervous of where this conversation was headed, I stood in wait. Kenton invited me over *to talk*. In our first post contract conversation he expressed his displeasure regarding speaking on the phone, and had always waited for me to make some type of contact with him. My uninvited arrivals at his home had become quite the norm.

"Victoria can cook like no other," he smiled, looked down, and smoothly swung his putter.

This was a very difficult twenty five foot putt on a surface which was far from flat. As the ball appeared to be headed three feet to the right of the cup he turned away. Now facing me and smiling, he raised his right hand to his ear and closed his eyes.

"Listen," he whispered.

I chose to watch.

As the golf ball topped the crest of the path it was traveling along, it began to gain speed and roll to the left. Now racing directly toward the cup, it was apparently on the right path all along. I grinned and continued to watch as Kenton stood with his hand to his ear and his eyes closed.

Ker-plunk.

"I love that sound," he breathed.

"It sure didn't *look* like it was headed in that direction," I shook my head in disbelief.

"It was an easy lie to read, Parker. I figured it'd break about three feet. It did," he said as he walked toward the cup.

"There was a number of ways for me to get there. None would have been wrong. Temperature, time of day, Downes' maintenance of the green, the force in which my putter makes contact with the ball," he paused as he pulled the ball from the cup.

"All of these things have an effect on the putt. We don't all read the green the same, Parker. But putting is like making the commitment to have sex. Everything has to be perfect, or it's just another stroke on your scorecard. Once you pull the trigger there's no changing things. So, take all the time you need to prepare. And when you commit, know deep in the pit of your gut it's what is right, because you only have one chance to do things properly."

Kenton providing me with advice regarding the sacred nature of sex felt hypocritical at first. As I stood and considered what he said, and the fact *he* said it, I placed more value on the statement. His advice was sound and solid. I suppose there's no one person more apt to provide accurate information on securing your home from a burglar than the burglar himself.

"I won't have sex with Victoria," I blurted.

"Ever?" he looked confused.

"Well, I shouldn't say *never*. But I won't until we're married," I rolled my shoulders forward and looked down at the surface of the green.

Feeling rather embarrassed, I stood quietly as I waited for Kenton to respond. Most don't understand or agree with saving sex for marriage. When people learn the existence of a twenty-three year old male virgin, they immediately claim he is a liar. Upon assurance the statement is an accurate one they assume there must be something wrong with him. It's virtually impossible for people in this day and age to digest such a thing.

Almost always, upon learning of my virginity, the remark is something along the line of *why?*

"Interesting. And, I must say, quite admirable," he paused mid-stride and nodded his head as he walked toward the shaded upper deck.

"It's how I was raised," I said proudly as I followed him toward the deck.

"By your grandmother?" he asked as he sat down.

I nodded my head, "Yes sir."

"You're a virgin?"

"Yes sir."

"And you expect you'll wait to have sex until you're married?"

"I don't *expect* I will. I'm quite certain of it. I owe it to my grandmother. And to myself, I suppose. I've waited this long, I'm not going to sacrifice a lifelong belief for an evening of pleasure."

"I admire you, Parker. I certainly do. So, how's long has it been?" he asked as he positioned his face over the pitcher of tea and inhaled a breath through his nose.

The thought of Kenton admiring me was very reassuring. It provided me with a sense of achievement and filled me with self-worth to think of someone such as Kenton admired me for my choices in life. In our time together, he always provided me with two things – sound advice and a warm feeling in my heart.

"Peach. Fabulous," he smiled as he raised the pitcher.

"What? How long?" I was confused by his question.

"How long have you been seeing Victoria now?"

"Oh, roughly seven weeks," I responded.

"Roughly seven?" he chuckled.

"Yes sir."

"Just a rough guess?" he smiled as he poured a glass of tea and pushed it across the table toward me.

"Seven weeks and three days, to be a little more exact," I laughed.

"Your thoughts, in summary?" he asked as he gazed into his glass of tea.

"Regarding her? Us?" I asked.

He nodded his head as he continued to appear distracted by the contents of his tea glass.

"Well, the same as before, I guess," I paused, wondering if there was anything new to offer since our last discussion.

"The fibers. The peach matter stays suspended in the liquid, like little floating hairs. It must be why I enjoy this so much more than the raspberry. The raspberries simply sink to the bottom of the pitcher," he shook his head as he looked up from the glass, "my apologies. Continue, please."

"I don't know if I have anything new to offer," I shrugged.

"Well, a reiteration will suffice. I enjoy hearing about you two immensely. Tell me about *the girl*, Parker. You're beginning to bore me," he chuckled.

"Well, her mother is dependent upon painkillers, an addiction that stemmed from an accident at work. One thing led to another, and she is now, in Victoria's own words, a slave to narcotics. Sad, when you think about it. Victoria seems to find at least some satisfaction in caring for her. She really doesn't complain about it. I think most would," I said.

"I agree. It speaks volumes of her devotion to family and loved ones," Kenton nodded his head as he leaned into the back of his chair and crossed his legs.

"There's not much I can tell you about her you don't already know. She loves to cook, but never does. She's a little bit of a wild one, and definately not afraid to toss an expletive into a conversation to prove a point or get your attention," I grinned and slowly shook my head.

"*Sit down, you big fucking brute, w*hen she said that I damn near pissed myself. You know, after you left that night, Downes and I talked at length. He told me he stood in the kitchen with her as she prepared the entire meal. It was at her insistence. She told him he intimidated her and she didn't like it. But, as intimidated as she was, she chose to face her fear. In a matter of thirty minutes, she learned Downes is nothing short of a true gentleman. He can be rather stern, but a gentlemen nonetheless. I'm truly pleased she made friends with him."

"She told me the same thing. She compared him to a well-trained German Shepherd – very protective over the people he loves, in a constant state of preparedness, and loyal until death. I had to admit I agreed with her," I looked through the French doors hoping to catch a glimpse of him, yet saw nothing but my own reflection.

"I meant what I said wholeheartedly," Kenton said as he leaned forward in his chair.

"Regarding?" I asked.

"Having dinner together made me feel like we were a family. It really did, and must say I enjoyed it immensely. I now yearn for it. I want you two to come here as much as possible. I've grown to love you, Parker. I truly have. And seeing you with Victoria," he paused, raised his hands to his face, and turned in the seat of his chair to face the ocean.

After a very long moment of silence, still facing the ocean, he began to speak.

"You know, we fear what we *don't* understand and find serenity in what we're *incapable* of understanding. I find tremendous satisfaction in this; staring out into the ocean, that is. It's endless. From what I can see from here, there is a well-defined beginning and no ending whatsoever. It just goes on forever. I find it...well, there's nothing else that compares, Parker. The tranquility from this viewpoint is immeasurable," as his voice began to falter, he inhaled an audible breath.

After an extended pause, he continued speaking.

"You and Victoria – how the two of you react and respond to each other is nothing short of magic. When I began this venture, I hoped to obtain a false sense of satisfaction that I had played a part in the forming of what could or would be a perfect relationship for someone. I had little hope, if any, that it would truly come to fruition. I expected to provide advice on gentlemanly behavior to someone who *needed* my guidance. You, son, need nothing. You're the last of a dying breed of men, you truly are. Short of you choosing to part ways with me, I can make this statement without reservation," he stood from his chair, gripped his putter, and looked down at the surface of the deck.

"I'll be here for you, wholeheartedly," he looked up from the deck, "until the bitter end."

As Kenton faced me, I immediately noticed his eyes were puffy and red. In staring out toward the ocean, he had probably become emotional over the thought of Victoria and me being part of his adopted family. Studying his face, it appeared as if he had been crying. The thought of him obtaining this level of satisfaction from the two of us caused me to realize not only was Kenton Ward human, he was also invested emotionally. He felt just as I did. He found value in having me be a part of his life no differently than I found value in having him be a part of mine. The entire idea of him employing me had seemed ludicrous at first. Now, sitting here, it made perfect sense. Kenton Ward was living a vicarious life through Victoria and me – one that he had been incapable of living himself.

"The bitter end being?" I asked, not necessarily wanting to know the answer.

"Life itself," he responded, extending his hand toward me.

As I stood and gripped his hand, it dawned on me. At this very moment, Kenton Ward and I were making a pact. He, at least in my mind, had adopted me as a member of his extended family, for a lifetime. Holding his hand firmly in mine, for the first time in my life, it was as if I was shaking the hand of my father.

Hand in hand, we stood silently and stared; both incapable of speaking.

And I began to weep.

VICTORIA

Parker caused me to feel.

Simply stated, I stand afraid I'll never be the same. I am forever ruined by his simple, caring, thoughtful, and often silent ways. Although I have never been in a position like this with a boy, and have little if anything to compare it to, I know Parker is special. It isn't merely my lack of experience in being exposed to the male species; it's the fact this particular male, of the entire species of males, stands out as being beyond exceptional.

For me, that is. I am not so foolish that I don't realize Parker may not be for everyone. To be quite candid, I reserve hope all other women he may expose himself to despise him and view his humility as pretentious, and consider him a prick. If this were the case, it would eliminate any potential female competition, and solidify my relationship with him.

I desperately want him to be in my life forever. Our relationship is perfect for me, but something most women, or men for that matter, would not understand. We don't have sex. We rarely kiss, and aren't overly affectionate, especially in the presence of others. What we have is nothing short of spectacular, but it isn't what most would perceive as *normal.*

There's a part of me, and it is growing like a lump of cancer, that wants to pull Parker's clothes off and fuck him into a coma. With each passing day, the desire grows. Some days it is far worse than others, but I fight it with every ounce of what I believe is my moral being. For me, sex will only come after marriage.

No exception.

I find one thing about Parker which is more satisfying than anything else. He is truly satisfied with what he receives from me, or to state more accurately, *doesn't receive from me*, sexually. Not only does he not desire more, he wouldn't accept it if I were to attempt to force it upon him.

In the parking lot of the restaurant, we had been sitting and talking for almost an hour. Although I really needed to get home and check on my mother, I felt it impossible to leave him. Sometimes, when I have to do something I really despise, I count to five and just do it when *five* comes.

"I could sit and listen to you talk about absolutely nothing and find tremendous satisfaction in doing so," he said softly as he raised my hair over my ear with his finger.

One.

"Thank you. I think. I like listening to you, too. It's like you're a mentally challenged mini Shakespeare. Not as eloquent, but far more fucking satisfying," I grinned.

Two.

"Mini Shakespeare. Why thank you. And I have no idea why, but I find it attractive when you curse," he smiled.

The street lights illuminated the interior of his car with blue-ish warmth. His facial features on the right were shadowed by the rear of the car, making him appear even handsome. As I studied his face and smiled, his index finger followed softly along my jawline. I closed my eyes softly and became hypnotized by his touch. As his finger reached the tip of my chin, I crossed my legs.

You better stop that shit, Parker Bale.

"Good fucking deal," I whispered, my eyes still closed.

Three.

"You need to stop touching me, you're driving me crazy," I breathed.

Four.

"And you, my dear, have driven me crazy since the day we first met. To imagine spending my life without you in it makes me feel ill. Whatever it is you're doing to me, it's working," he said softly.

Five.

Fuck.

"I have to go, I'm sorry. My mother..." I opened my eyes and felt along the door for the door handle.

"I understand," he responded.

As he opened his door and walked toward my side of the car, I grinned. When he was a few feet from my door, I pulled the handle, opened it, and stepped onto the surface of the parking lot.

"Why can't you wait for me to open the door for you?" he asked.

"I can. I like screwing with you," I smiled.

Cautiously, he wrapped his arms around my waist and pulled me into his chest. Softly, I lowered my head to his shoulder and closed my eyes. This was the time I so looked forward to. *The touching.* Although I yearned for it always, it came when I needed it the most; immediately prior to our departures. Having it continue in this manner allowed me to practice and exercise resistance to further sexual advancements. As I inhaled a shallow breath of his cologne I felt as if I was growing.

"What did you mean? The *whatever you're doing to me, it's working* comment?" I asked as I opened my eyes.

With his hands clasped behind me, continuing to hold my waist to his, he leaned away from me and looked into my eyes.

"*You make me weak*, that's what I meant. By merely being, Victoria. You make me weak," he whispered.

I smiled.

"And you, Parker Bale, make me feel strong – more and more with each passing day. When you hold me in your arms, I feel as if I'm growing. Odd but true."

He leaned forward and encompassed my lower lip between his and kissed me deeply. My entire body tingling, I pressed against his shoulders, slowly pulling free of his kiss.

"See? Strength," I said as I gripped my clutch in my right hand.

I shook my head and smiled, "I damned sure need it to leave a kiss like that. Goodnight, love."

I continued to shake my head as I walked toward my car. I unlocked my car and tossed my clutch into the passenger seat. As I looked over the top of the car toward him, he acted as if he fainted against the side of his car. I rolled my eyes and waited anxiously to see what he had to say.

As he stood up straight, he grinned, "See? Weak."

My elbows resting on the top of my car, I smiled, "We're perfect for each other."

And in my heart of hearts I knew that to be true.

VICTORIA

"You should turn the television down, mother. It's so loud," I suggested as I walked past her.

She looked up from her position in the chair as I walked by, but offered nothing in response to my statement. In recent weeks, her dependency of narcotics and reliance on my provision of them was becoming rather stressful. I'm sure my having lost my job and the amount of time I was now spending with Parker wasn't helping matters. Stress always brings on a change in attitude with me, which in turn manufactures more stress. Frustrated with my mother's condition, I shook my head and stepped into the hallway.

"I'm going to shower and go try to find a job," I screamed into the living room.

She reached for the bottle of OxyContin on the table beside her. As she fumbled with the lid of the bottle, I shouted again. It seemed as if the extent of our communication had become small bursts of shouting and never an actual discussion of any nature. What Parker and I had developed provided me with a sense of peacefulness I have never felt here. My interactions with my mother had become much more torturous since meeting Parker.

"I said I'm going to shower," I hollered.

"I heard you," she yelled as the lid snapped from the top of the bottle, dumping the contents into her lap.

I rolled my eyes as I turned to walk into the living room and pick up the mess of pills. Something as simple as opening a bottle had become difficult for her in recent months, it was as if her need for the narcotics had become greater, or her pain had worsened. Either way, she was now in a more medicated state and her motor skills were deteriorating.

"I'm fine. I'm a grown woman, Victoria. I don't need you to do *everything* for me. Take your shower and go get a job," she bellowed as soon as she realized I was walking in her direction.

"Mother," I sighed.

"Don't *mother* me, Victoria Lillian," she hissed.

"Fine," I huffed.

For me, nothing has ever compared to taking a shower. From a relaxation standpoint, life couldn't possibly offer anything greater than warm beads of water beating against my naked body. The sense of security I felt in the shower was second to none. Or me, it was a reminder that this was my time alone, and as long as I stood in the water, I was alone and would remain alone. The warmth of the water softened me mentally and allowed me to find a tranquil state I was incapable of finding elsewhere. Since childhood, I have always looked forward to my time in the bath or shower, and I often showered twice a day. Generally, I would stand in the stream of water and sing until there was no hot water remaining.

Today was no exception.

As I patted my hair dry, I considered what I may wear to meet Parker and Kenton for lunch. Something about being in Kenton's home caused me to feel as if I needed to dress up, and not wear my typical casual attire. I've never looked at myself as ugly, and I haven't felt I lack self-esteem, but dressing up always made me feel a little *more* beautiful. As I pressed the towel into my skin, I mentally dressed myself.

The little dress I bought for my job interview would look cute. It was a few years old now, but I had only worn it once. I could wear it with my little flats I got at the mall last year. It would at least look to my mother like I was going to look for a job, and not going to lunch.

Draped in a damp towel, I walked through the living room toward my bedroom. *Jerry Springer* blared from the television. I didn't need to see or hear what was on the television to know exactly what was happening.

Someone was screwing someone else's girlfriend, and there would definitely be a baby involved. One of the two male hillbillies, the one emotionally committed to the trashy female, would succumb to a DNA test. After a commercial break, he would find out he was not the father of the child. A fight would ensue, and be broken up by the staff just prior to the knockout punch. The crowd would cheer through the entire debacle for more. Angry, I shut my bedroom door and provided what little barrier I could to filter the noise as I got dressed.

Ridiculous.

To think my mother's life had become *this* – permanently positioned deep in her recliner, high on narcotics, fumbling for her next pill as she watched yet another episode of Jerry Springer. I yearned for something normal with her, but was well aware life with her would more than likely bring nothing more than this.

Unless something changed.

I often visualized that one day I would come home and find her in the kitchen cooking dinner. In the dream, she would announce to me although the pain was still noticeable, she felt it could be managed. Later, after a few days of living in a lesser medicated state, she would realize she was nothing more than an addict, and accept my suggestion to receive some type of treatment for her addiction. After a thirty day treatment program, she would emerge a different person.

I wanted to introduce Parker to her, and have her accept him as being who he was to me. To do so now would be an exercise in futility and an embarrassing situation for me. Frustrated, I got dressed and looked in the mirror on the back of my bedroom door.

Beautiful, simply beautiful.

Eager to meet Parker and see Kenton and Downes again, I opened my door and walked toward the bathroom. *Fifteen minutes and I'll be out of here.* It's strange how things change in life. Before Parker, I had no reason to do anything but read, work, and take care of my mother. Although I was never satisfied with my mother's state of being, I was not as frustrated as I am now. I was at that point in time, however, satisfied with my life as a whole. Now, my annoyance with her condition was at an all-time high, and I wanted her to change. I hoped for a normal life with Parker, and to have any resemblance of that with her in *this* state was nothing short of impossible.

"Will you at least turn it down enough that I can't hear it over the hair dryer?" I asked as I walked past.

Nothing.

I turned to face her and in doing so realized she was asleep. It wasn't uncommon for her to fall asleep immediately after taking a pill. It was as if the initial jolt of whatever the narcotics provided was just too much, and it would cause her to pass out. After an hour long nap, she would awaken in a more medicated state, sometimes angry she had missed a portion or all of whatever was blaring away on the television. Quietly, I stepped into the room, turned down the television, and placed the remote control in her lap beside her hand.

Silence.

Pleased at the sound of *nothing*, I walked in the bathroom and shut the door. After fifteen minutes, my hair was dry, curled, and my make-up done. I've never used a tremendous amount of make-up, and always felt the less I used the better I looked. We all, however, need *something*.

Satisfied my only improvement could be to have Parker by my side, I opened the bathroom door.

Silence.

Feeling frustrated with her in general but fractionally guilty for not telling her the absolute truth about my whereabouts for the afternoon, I walked into the living room to tell her goodbye. I lowered my lips to her forehead and kissed her gently, being careful not to wake her. Her skin felt cool against my warm lips.

Probably her lowered heart rate.

I kissed her again.

This isn't normal.

I brushed her hair aside and kissed her again.

"Mother, I'm leaving," I pressed my hands against her upper arms and softly shook her.

"Mom," I pressed harder.

"No. No. No. Don't do this," I reached behind her shoulders and tried to help her sit up in the chair.

The sheer weight of her body prevented me from lifting her from the seat. I released her shoulders and pressed my hand against her forehead. It felt cold against my palm, but not *that* cold. Frantic, I unzipped my clutch, pulled out my phone, and made two phone calls.

"Nine one one, do you have an emergency?" the operator asked.

"Yes. It's my mother. She isn't responding and she feels kind of cool."

"Your address. What is your address, ma'am?"

"648 Wichita Ave, El Cajon. She won't. She doesn't respond."

"Ma'am, I'll dispatch an ambulance immediately. When did she last show signs of responding or speak to you?"

"Uhmm. After. After I took my…no I mean before. I'm sorry, I'm nervous. It was before my shower. Maye thirty minutes ago."

"Is she taking any medications or did she ingest anything that you're aware of? Does she have any allergies?"

"She uhhm. She just took an OxyContin. Or I think she did. She was taking one when I was getting into the shower. I asked her to turn the T.V. down. Can you hurry? She doesn't feel really cold, just kind of cold. Like just not really normal."

"Does she have a history of using pain killers, ma'am?"

"Yes. She had an accident at work. She takes them daily. Can you hurry?"

"Yes, ma'am. They're en route now. It'll be a few minutes. Are you near her now?"

"Yes, I'm standing here in the living room."

"Softly open her eyelid and describe her pupil, the black center portion of her eye. Let me know if it's large or small. Are you comfortable doing that for me?"

"Yes, just a minute."

"It's tiny. Is that normal? Is it supposed to be big?"

"The pupils dilate ma'am. They change from large to small, back and forth, depending on medical condition. I'm simply collecting data. Is your house number visible from the street? And can you describe the house to me?"

"It's kind of greyish. The garage is on the right. There's an alley on the right side of the garage that leads to the school behind us. It's more of a walk way. My car is in the driveway. It's an old school Celica."

"Toyota Celica, ma'am? And what year and color?""

"Yes, it's a Toyota. 1978. Yellowish. Faded yellow."

"I need to call Parker. Can I call you back?"

"I'd like to keep you on the phone, ma'am."

"I really need to call him, can I call you back? They're coming, right?"

"The ambulance is en route, ma'am. If you'd like to hang up, I'll call you in two minutes. Six one nine four four seven one zero three five?"

"Uhhm. Yes. Six one nine four four seven one zero three five."

"Parker, it's me. There's an emergency, I'm sorry I'm late."

"Are you okay?"

"Yes, I'm okay, it's my mom. She's had a reaction or something. She isn't responding."

"What's your address?"

"It's okay, they're sending an ambulance, I don't need…"

"Victoria. What's your address?"

"It's all the way in El Cajon. I don't need…"

"Victoria. What is it?"

"648 Wichita Avenue."

"I'll be there as soon as I can get there."

"Okay, I need to go. The operator's calling me back in a minute."

"I'll be there soon, Victoria."

"Victoria?"

"Yeah?"

"I love you."

"I love you too, Parker."

As the sound of the distant ambulance grew louder, I stepped beside my mother's chair and carefully picked up the loose pills from her lap. One by one, I dropped them into the bottle and secured the lid. Slowly, I walked into the bathroom, opened the medicine cabinet, and placed the bottle on the shelf.

She'll need those as soon as she wakes up.

PARKER

I had no expectation of Victoria's mother dying so soon. I suspect my position regarding death is probably different than most other people – I view death as the last chapter in the book of life – the ending if you will. I've made the comparison many times. It's difficult to judge a book or give an honest opinion about a story until you've *completed* reading it. Prior to the formulation of the ending, it's nothing more than a series of events as expressed in a number of various chapters. Upon completion, the ending ties everything together and turns all which preceded it into a finished story. The ending has the ability to make or break a story, and typically wraps everything up with a nice little bow, allowing a series of highlighted events to come together and make perfect sense as a whole. In the absence of the ending, it's simply an unfinished story. Death is the completion of life, the ending of the book. As a wise woman once said, *from our feeble beginning, through all of the complications, and to what will certainly be an unscheduled and unwelcome ending, life happens.*

An unscheduled and unwelcome ending. They're all unscheduled and unwelcome when you think about it. Having an understanding of this doesn't necessarily make it easy for everyone to digest, but for me, dying was part of life itself. It had been two days since her mother's death, and it seemed Victoria was either in a state of denial or a state of relief regarding the matter. She had not yet shown any signs of remorse, which troubled me. I desperately wanted to comfort her, but so far she appeared to need nothing from me to help her through this. Kenton seemed more troubled regarding the death than anyone, and as I wasn't capable of providing Victoria with any form of relief, my current focus was Kenton.

"I worry about her Parker," he sighed.

"So do I. But at least for now she appears to be doing rather well," I responded.

"That she does. It doesn't change the fact that the time will come when she needs someone, someone to be there for her, comfort her, and provide for her. She needs to know you're always available. I don't want her to need and not have," he said over the top of his menu.

"She won't, I'll always be here and I have made it crystal clear. And she knows," I nodded.

"I know she does. I'm rambling, my apologies. Everyone handles death differently. Maybe she handles it better than most, who knows," he placed the menu on the table and looked over his shoulder for the non-existent waitress.

"Well, her father passed when she was an infant, and now her mother. It doesn't sound as if she's had too much exposure to death. Not having an active father and growing up in a home without him was a constant reminder of just how permanent death is, but that doesn't make *understanding* it easy," I said as I scanned the room for the waitress.

Kenton began to cough, and as he covered his mouth, he looked down and around the table. As he shook his head in apparent disbelief, I realized we were not only were we missing a waitress, but we were without anything to drink.

"I never knew my father, and my mother died of breast cancer when I was in my mid-thirties. It's almost as if we've all been drawn together by an outside force to comfort each other with strength gained from our experiences. When was she planning on showing up?" he asked as he glanced at his watch.

"Three-thirty or so," I responded.

"It's twelve now. We have plenty of time, but this is ridiculous," he said as he attempted to clear his throat.

"It is. So, your mother died of cancer?" I asked, shocked this was the first I'd heard of it.

"She did. And my father was a man I never had the opportunity to meet," he said as he rested his elbow on the table and tapped his lip with his index finger.

"My grandmother died of cancer, I'm sure you remember. She was basically my mother, you know. I never knew she had it. I always felt if I had known, maybe there would have been something I could have done. Not knowing, in some respects made it easier, I suppose. I'm sorry to hear about your mother," I said softly.

"I knew about my mother's cancer, and it was a harrowing experience. A very heartbreaking struggle filled with excruciating pain for both of us. I wouldn't wish the type or degree of pain I felt during that time upon anyone. I'm certain hers was much worse. And trust me – there would have been nothing you could have done to change things. I tried. No amount of money can change the course once it's set. Excuse me," he said as he stood from his chair and walked away.

After a quick scan around the dining area for who I suspected was the waitress, he turned and walked toward the entrance of the restaurant. Almost immediately, he returned to the room where we were seated followed by a waiter. As he lowered himself into his seat, he tilted his head to the side as if there was something he wished to say. After a few seconds passed, he merely shook his head and remained silent.

"I'm sorry gentlemen, we're short-staffed. I'm Shane; I'll be your waiter. Can I get you something to drink? Wine, beer, tea, soda, water?" the waiter said cheerily.

"I'll have iced tea, and I'd like to order as well," Kenton sighed as he looked at his watch.

"Go right ahead sir," said the waiter.

"I want the fried octopus, but not as an appetizer, bring it with the meal, please. And for lunch, I'll have the pine crusted whitefish, the special," Kenton picked his menu from the table and held it in his hand as he spoke.

"I'll make it easy, I'll have the same," I smiled.

"And to drink?" the waiter asked.

Apparently still frustrated, Kenton raised one eyebrow and turned to face the waiter.

"Tea, I'll have the tea as well," I chuckled as I handed Kenton my menu.

"Alright, and now as far as iced tea goes, we have the black tea, green tea, and today we have peach tea," the waiter smiled.

Simultaneously, Kenton and I responded.

"Peach."

"Peach."

"Peach it is," the waiter said as he pulled the menus from Kenton's grasp.

"Have you tried the octopus here?" Kenton asked as the waiter walked away.

"I have not. Actually, I've never eaten here."

"They're simply marvelous. They'll all be tiny, fried up and served on a plate. Like a family. They're the babies, I guess. The bodies range in size from about the size of a nickel to the size of a quarter. And the legs are like pieces of twine. They cook them whole here. They're considerably more tasteful than the chopped up pieces, which I refuse to eat. I've never known why, but I don't like thinking about eating their tentacles alone. It reminds me of eating an arm. For the same reason, I won't eat a chicken leg. The thought of it seems savage. But I have no concerns eating their arms as long as they're attached to their bodies. Go figure," he laughed.

"Maybe it's about sacrifice and commitment," I responded.

"How so," he asked.

"Well, if you have a chicken leg or a chopped up octopus tentacle on a plate, you really don't know about what happened to or with the rest of the animal. It could have been a torturous affair, the removal of its limb. But, if the entire animal is on the plate, even though it didn't have a say in the matter, it's all there. It's as if the octopus committed itself to you, entirely. It made the sacrifice to be served as a meal," I nodded my head, satisfied I had made the point I intended to.

"Sacrifice, I like that. I'd say you may have something there, Parker. I like how your mind works. You're a thinker," he chuckled.

As Kenton laughed, the waiter arrived with a tray containing our entire order. As he lowered the tray to the elevation of the table, Kenton tilted his head toward the waiter.

"Well, *that* was fast," Kenton said, "I was afraid I would expire from this cough before you returned."

"We're always fast at lunch time, sir. Maybe not to *take* the order, but to *prepare* it, yes," he began to place the food and beverages on the table as he spoke.

"Anything else?" the waiter asked.

"No thank you," Kenton responded.

Kenton quickly took a drink of tea and cleared his throat. In looking down at the octopus, Kenton's facial expression turned to one of disgust. As he studied the plate, he slid it to the side and pulled the plate of fish in front of him.

"For some reason, I can't do it today. It's too much a reminder of the entire death thing. I'm becoming a softie, Parker," he said as he shook his head lightly.

I slid the platter of octopus across the table until it was positioned directly in front of me.

"I ordered them, and I'm going to eat them. I know they didn't run out and catch them solely to prepare my meal, but it's just…well, I don't want these little fellows to have made the ultimate sacrifice for nothing. I think we all die for a reason, and *they* died so we can eat them, there's no other reason I can really think of. If I eat them, it's completes the cycle, and they've died for a reason. If not, their death was meaningless. And I believe everything happens for a reason, including death. Sometimes it's difficult to interpret, but with these little guys, at least I understand why," I chuckled as I picked one of the fried delicacies from the plate and plopped it into my mouth.

"Here's to *not* dying a meaningless death," Kenton laughed as he pulled the plate of fried octopus in front of the fish.

And, although we had been laughing over the death of a fried octopus, something about the lunch with Kenton gave me hope. Hope that Victoria's mother had not died without there being some form of greater reason, one I was currently incapable of seeing. I realize life isn't always for me to understand, but I do feel a responsibility to regularly practice acceptance.

"You know, they say when you drop a lobster into a pot of boiling water, they scream. You think these little guys suffered, Parker?" Kenton laughed as he picked one from the plate.

"Absolutely not," I responded as I picked a perfectly sized one from the plate.

And at that particular moment, it made sense – perfect sense – at least to me.

Suffering.

Victoria's mother was no longer going to suffer, nor was Victoria. They were both now free of their bindings. Her mother had, in a sense, beaten her drug addiction and was no longer in agony. And Victoria should be able live with the comfort knowing she cared for her mother until her death. Satisfied, I looked down at the last octopus lying on my plate.

"Here's to understanding why," I said as I lifted it from the plate.

"Amen," Kenton nodded.

The suffering has ended.

Amen.

PARKER

Six days had passed since the death of Victoria's mother. Although Victoria didn't appear to go through a noticeable grieving process, I'm quite certain she grieved or continues to grieve in her own way. She didn't cry at the funeral service, a small affair over an urn of ashes in which the funeral home director gave the eulogy to a small and somber group. I, on the other hand, found the funeral to be quite sad. Based on the lack of attendance during the service, it was apparent there was very little interest in her mother's death.

Or her life.

Kenton, Downes, Victoria, one neighbor and I comprised the entire wake.

The value of a person's life is measured by the amount of people they touch in living it. Based on this belief, I have always further believed a person's funeral would be a depiction of the perceived value in the life they've lived – the means of measure being the people in attendance at the funeral – the touched souls.

For that reason, and that reason alone, I found the funeral of Victoria's mother to be rather unsettling. Throughout the service, I tried to think of the people who would attend *my* funeral. I made a conscious count of people I was satisfied would attend, and added others which *may* be in attendance. The result was humbling and almost as unsettling as the funeral service itself.

The total amount – six – caused me to feel regret for the life I have lived to date. Although I have attempted and continue to pursue living a life with no regrets regarding my behavior or beliefs, I have a very small circle of people who know me, love me, or have been touched by something I have said or done.

Frustrated and somewhat disappointed with myself, I sat in the service and looked over the small seating area. *Downes, Victoria, Kenton, the deceased, and some unknown neighbor.* With each person, I attempted to do the same – count the people who I believed would be in attendance of *their* funeral. With Kenton and Victoria, I believed the number to be a small one. With the others, I was incapable of guessing accurately. Based on the assumption the unknown persons had a family, I suspected the number to be considerably higher.

As I counted and recounted I began to become saddened by the fact Victoria, Kenton and I had no family. We only had each other. We would be required to develop a family of our own through reproduction, friends, associates, and those we touched through the course of living our lives.

Life is easy. Live it while you're alive.

Because when you're gone you won't have an opportunity.

As the funeral director continued speaking, I held Victoria's hand. Slowly, I slid my free hand from the armrest of my seat and onto Kenton's left forearm. As my hand moved toward his wrist, he turned to face me, smiled lightly, and gripped my hand in his. And, as I held the hands of what little family I had, I closed my eyes made a vow.

To begin living life.

While I was alive.

VICTORIA

I gripped the handrail in my palms as I stared out at the horizon. The light morning breeze blew the smell of the beach into my face, providing me with a feeling of relaxation in an almost magical sense. Slowly it faded away, and with it, my gratification. Eager for its return, I closed my eyes and inhaled softly through my nose.

Crap, that never works.

I will always find the unexpected scent of lilacs filling my nostrils while jogging through the park much more rewarding than forcing my nose into a bouquet and inhaling the same essence. One is encountered unexpectedly, as if it were provided as a gift; and the other taken. Personally, I prefer provision to theft.

Often when there's scent or soft aroma I enjoy, I'll attempt to take a shallow breath to savor it even more. Invariably, the scent disappears in my eager effort to inhale it – a simple reminder of the fact that some things happen naturally, and if we attempt to force them, they'll simply fade away. I believe the natural scents of this earth come as a gift from God, evidence when we need it the most, of his existence. When we need a reminder, he provides. If we attempt to obtain them through coercion, we question his existence; and they disappear.

"There's a fresh pitcher of tea here, and I must say it's even better than the last," Kenton's voice was soft, almost as if he were speaking to a child.

I loosened my grip on the handrail and closed my eyes, hoping for the scent of the beach to return. As I listened to the seagulls singing their songs along the beach, I became one with them, flying over the ocean without a single thought. My wings spread, the soft breeze keeping me afloat above all of the others, I soared.

"Are you hungry yet?" Parker asked.

I opened my eyes and gripped the handrail tightly for a brief second as I took an aggravated shallow breath. As I released my grip, I turned to face the table where Kenton, Parker, and now Downes were seated. Downes smiled as I looked up. Kenton and Parker's faces were both filled with signs of wonder.

My mother began dying a slow death, one I was certain to be much more rapid than typical, the day my father died. I further believe a part of her died each and every day she lived without him. He was, at her admittance, her only love. She had never loved before, and certainly didn't after. In retrospect, the painkillers she became reliant upon provided her ability to eliminate the pain associated with his absence from our lives.

As time passed, I grew older and she became more tolerant to the effects of the pills, requiring more of them to provide shelter from the pain. Her realization of my growth was a constant reminder that one day I too may fall in love, and move forward with my life, leaving her in pain and alone. Her death was inevitable, not a matter of *if*, but a matter of *when*.

I feel sorrow for my mother no longer being in my life, but I am not sorry she has moved on. I am of the belief she can now, in mind and possibly in spirit, be with the man she loved – living a life she would be incapable of living on this earth.

"Are you hungry yet?" Parker asked again.

"You two are driving me fucking nuts," I snapped.

"Who? These two?" Parker asked as he motioned to Downes and Kenton.

"No, Parker. You and Kenton. *Jesus*. Victoria, do you want this? Victoria do you want that? Can I get you anything? Do you need anything? How do you feel? Did you sleep well last night? No. No. No. No. Great. And not exactly," I said as I began walking their direction, shaking my head in disbelief as I approached.

"It's because we care," Parker sighed.

"And I *know* you care. I do. You don't have to prove it. My mother's dead, and I'm okay with it. Can you two be okay that I'm okay? Kenton, you're mother's dead. Parker, yours is too. But I'm not coddling you, trying to force you to drink another gallon of tea hoping it will drown the pain," I rolled my eyes and flopped into the chair across the table from where Parker and Kenton were seated.

"Are you in pain?" Parker asked.

"No. *Jesus fucking Christ.* I'm not in pain, Parker. I'm the opposite, I'm in love. I want to hug and kiss and lay with you in my arms, not wallow in non-existent grief. Please, for the love of God, *stop*. Accept the fact that I believe, and I truly do," frustrated, I paused and ran my hands through my hair.

"My mother is in a better place. I know that sounds cheesy or cliché or whatever, but I *believe* that. I don't believe it because it's easy or because it's a way for me to *get by* without coping with her death. I believe it because I believe it – deep down in my core of beliefs. Or whatever. *Fuck*. How about Downes and I go make you two grieving pricks a sandwich and get you another gallon of tea?" as I finished speaking, I realized I was standing again.

Parker and Kenton's faces filled with shock, they sat with their mouths agape. Downes sat quietly, unsuccessfully fighting an urge to smile. Still rather frustrated, but feeling quite satisfied with my speech, I smiled, tilted my head, and tossed my hair. As I alternated glances between Kenton and Parker, I gripped the edge of the table with my hands and raised my eyebrows slowly.

Silence.

"Based on your silence, I assume we're done with this discussion?" I asked as my eyes darted back and forth between Kenton and Parker.

Kenton stood slowly, rubbing his lower back as he appeared to wince in pain.

As he opened his arms, he smiled, "My back is killing me, come here and give me a hug, my dear,"

I stepped to where he stood and wrapped my arms around him. As he held me in his arms, a light citrus scent of his unidentifiable cologne filled my nostrils. He always smelled the same, clean and soft. After a long moment, he leaned away, kissed the top of my head, and pressed his hands against my shoulders.

"I love you, Victoria," he said, smiling as he finished speaking.

"I love you too," I replied.

And I truly did.

I lowered my face into his chest and allowed him to hold me again. I had truly come to love Kenton. He was an unselfish man with unselfish ways. According to Parker, Kenton had lived a miserable life of self-importance years ago. Now, however, no signs of his former life remained. His allowing Parker and me to come and go from his home as we wished provided me with a sense of satisfaction I had never previously known. As my relationship with Parker developed, Kenton's home had slowly become my home away from home. Now, it seemed to be my *only* home. The view of the ocean was magnificent, and I frequently found comfort staring out into its endlessness.

As he held me in his arms, he rocked back and forth lightly on his heels. Slowly, my frustration faded away. Lost in the comfort of Kenton holding me, my breathing became shallow and without effort.

And my nostrils flared as the scent of the beach returned.

PARKER

Although I viewed my relationship with Victoria as being without fault, I found myself wanting more. The desire was not driven by greed or feeling of necessity for something I *wasn't* receiving, but solely by my love for her and the gratification I felt in – and out of – her presence. I was beginning to wonder if the feelings which would have developed naturally were accelerated by the absence of her mother, and Victoria's need for someone to accompany her through the course of merely living life.

Either way, I continued to feel as if what I was providing Victoria was insufficient. Feelings of inadequacy filled me in Victoria's absence; and in her presence, I was fulfilled. I had truly come to believe living a life without her was not a viable option. Incapable of seeing much, if any, benefit from continuing at the pace we were currently living our life of love, I opted to sit with the man who had proven to have all of the answers, and speak freely.

"But I don't want you to chastise me for my thoughts. I want to speak until I've exhausted myself before you chime in with whatever your beliefs may be, good or bad," I sighed.

"Agreed, you have my word. Is everything okay, son?" Kenton asked.

"Yes, quite alright. Just let me think for a minute, I'm flustered and nervous," I muttered as I pressed myself deeper into the loveseat.

I glanced around the room and thought of how to begin. The comfort I felt sitting in this room was unbelievable, especially considering the first time I entered it, I was afraid to even sit down. The same room where Kenton and I had shared our first sandwich together had become a second home for Victoria and me. Our invasion into Kenton's home, albeit invited, caused me to consider recommending he replace his front door with a revolving one.

Kenton leaned into the arm of the overstuffed chair which was, in my mind at least, *his*. Everything else in the living quarters of his home had, over time, become *ours*. Looking around the room, gratitude for what our relationship had become filled me, and I smiled.

As I wallowed nervously in the seat, I remembered my grandmother's advice.

If you have something you feel a need to say, simply say it. Anything more causes you to look foolish and indecisive.

"I want to marry Victoria," I blurted.

That didn't quite come out like I had planned.

Kenton jumped from his seat as if he'd been electrocuted.

Wait a minute, I need to back up, let me explain.

Almost immediately, he covered his mouth with his hand and began to bounce up and down. He resembled a four year old boy who desperately needed to pee and couldn't find a place to do so. As he continued to bounce, his mouth still covered by his hand, I began to wonder if he was alright.

"Well, say *something*. Are you alright?" I asked as I sat up in the loveseat.

Instantly, he pulled his hand away from his mouth, "Can I speak? You're done? Open discussion time?"

I inhaled deeply, and spoke upon exhaling, "I uhhm. I suppose…"

"Yes," I said nervously.

"Say it again, slowly," he said as he held his visibly shaking hands at his side.

"Say it again? What?" I asked, confused.

"What you said about Victoria. Say it again, please, slowly," he said excitedly.

Now feeling more nervous than before, I wondered if he misunderstood what I had previously said. I lowered myself into the seat and cleared my throat.

"I, uhhm. I want to marry Victoria," I said softly.

He began to bounce again.

And then he screamed a blood curdling scream.

"Downes! Get in here, we have an announcement. Parker has an announcement. Parker *and I* have an announcement. Hurry the fuck up!" he screamed.

I had never heard Kenton curse that I could recall. I wasn't really ready to talk to Downes regarding this matter, I felt as if there needed to be more one on one time with Kenton. Although I was proud of what Victoria and I had and how I felt, I wasn't prepared to tell the world, at least not just yet. Kenton, on the other hand, obviously felt much differently.

"No. No Downes. *Not yet*, Kenton," I shook my head lightly as I stood from my seat.

I no more than spoke, and Downes rushed into the room.

"What is it, Mr. Ward?" his eyes darted throughout the room as if they were on swivels.

"False alarm," Kenton huffed.

With all of the bouncing, Kenton was clearly out of breath. Still in shock over the cursing, screaming, Kenton's level of excitement, and not being certain of what his actual thoughts were regarding my announcement, I stood nervously and smiled.

"Mr. Ward? I think I'll go see a movie if it's alright," Downes raised his eyebrows and spoke in a stern tone.

"Oh Christ, seriously? Uhhm. Jesus, Downes, my memory has escaped me...," Kenton paused, placed his hands on his thighs, and stared at the floor.

Still heaving for his next breath, Kenton looked up and smiled, "*Five Easy Pieces.*"

"Very well. I'll be in the kitchen if you need me," Downes sighed, turned toward me, and smiled.

After Downes exited the room, Kenton rolled his eyes and sat down into his chair as he attempted to catch his breath. As his breathing slowed, he took a deep breath, exhaled, and grinned. Confused, I stood and stared at Kenton.

"At Downes insistence, we agreed to have a phrase only he and I would know. If he asked and I didn't provide the answer, he would know I was in truly in trouble. With all of the screaming and such, I'm certain he developed wonder. Okay, where were we?" Kenton asked as he began to rub his palms together.

I walked to the loveseat and lowered myself into the cushion. Proudly, I sat up in my seat and arched my back. After clearing my throat lightly and pausing for effect, I spoke.

"I said I wanted to marry Victoria."

He looked down into his lap and raised his hands to his face. After a moment, he looked up and used his index finger to wipe tears from his face. After alternating from cheek to cheek several times, he stopped crying and wiped his hands on his shorts.

"My apologies for the outburst earlier, I was excited. Now that things have settled, let me see," he hesitated and rubbed his palms back and forth rapidly.

"Fatherly advice. You need fatherly advice. Let me collect my wits. Dear God, I'm making a fool of myself. Parker, you've made me a mess," he sighed as he stood from his chair.

Slowly and methodically, he began to pace the room.

"Something as sacred as marriage should always be done as a result of what one feels in their heart, and never out of feelings of necessity or sorrow," he stopped pacing and looked in my direction.

"I love her, Kenton. That will never change. It won't fade, either. I'm certain," I responded proudly.

"Splendid, she's a fine woman. None finer, I'll say. Not a one," he smiled.

He began to pace again as he thought.

"Although in this day and age people seem to view it differently, marriage is a commitment for life, Parker. The union between the two of you will never be perfect. There will be times when you'll naturally want to walk out. Throw in the towel, so to speak. Everyone has them," he stopped pacing and raised his hand to his chin.

As he rubbed his chin between his index finger and thumb, he began to speak again.

"Surrender in marriage is not an option, Parker. It's certainly not. Communication is instrumental for a relationship to flourish. You must help her come to understand there will never be anything short of an open line of communication between you. No repercussion for speaking one's mind, ever."

"Understood, and I agree," I nodded.

"Monogamy, Parker. A monogamous relationship is the only relationship that has the ability to last. If you stray from this marriage, mark my words, I'll..." his voice filled with anger as he spoke.

"It'll never happen. You have my word," I interrupted before he finished speaking.

"When a man gives his word, he holds the world's perception of himself in his own palm," he faced me and pressed his hands into the pockets of his shorts.

"Kenton, she's the one," I hesitated and thought of the analogy Kenton had told me several months prior regarding playing cards.

I stood from my seat and cleared my throat. Kenton continued to stand in the center of the room, his hands pressed deeply into the pockets of his shorts. As I stood from my seat, he tilted his hear rearward and waited for what I chose to stand and offer him. I lowered the tone of my voice and attempted to mimic Kenton.

"You must know, and know you must, when to hold your cards close to your chest and say, *I'll risk it all*. Being so certain that what you're holding is *right*. That it is, without a doubt, the clear winner. So sure that you're willing to risk it all, everything you have, *knowing* you have a winner in your hands," I paused and smiled.

"Kenton, *I'm all in*. I'm willing to bet it all. And rest assured, I'll treat her with nothing but honor," I said proudly.

"When a man treats a woman with honor, it is a testament to the honor of the woman who raised him. I'm sorry I never had an opportunity to meet your grandmother. You make me proud, son," he said as he opened his arms.

As I opened my arms and stepped toward him, he lurched forward and lifted me from my feet.

"May I go with you to pick out the ring?" he asked as he squeezed me tightly in his arms.

"I suppose so," I coughed as he patted me sharply on the back with his hand.

As he broke the embrace, he raised his hand to his face again, wiping a tear from his cheek. To my surprise, I had yet to shed a tear during this discussion. Remarkably, it had gone much better than expected.

"May I call Downes, now?" Kenton asked.

"Absolutely," I smiled.

"Downes," Kenton hollered.

After a brief wait, Downes stepped into the room.

"Pull the B7 from the garage, please," Kenton smiled.

"The B7, Mr. Ward?" Downes asked.

Kenton nodded eagerly, "Yes sir."

I knew enough about Kenton and his cars to know the B7 was his prized possession as far as cars were concerned. It was a two year old BMW sedan which he had only driven roughly one thousand miles over the course of his ownership. The car cost approximately one hundred and sixty thousand dollars new. To say he drove the car on special occasions was an understatement.

"Special occasion, Mr. Ward?" Downes asked.

Kenton looked my direction and raised his eyebrows slightly. I nodded my head once, authorizing him to make the announcement.

"We'll be shopping for a ring, Downes, of the diamond variety. And to be honest, I'm too damned excited to drive. Care to?" Kenton asked as he pushed his hands into the pockets of his shorts.

"I'd be honored," Downes nodded his head toward Kenton then turned my direction, "I couldn't be more pleased, Mr. Bale."

"Thank you," I smiled.

As Downes walked from the room to retrieve the car, Kenton continued to nervously pace back and forth across the floor.

"Have you decided when and where you'll propose?" he asked.

I smiled and nodded my head eagerly.

"I have an idea and I think it just might be perfect…"

"Do tell," he said, his voice filled with excitement.

"You'll find out soon enough," I smiled.

And soon enough he would.

VICTORIA

As a child, I couldn't compare myself to other girls, because I wasn't *like* other girls. From the time I was a young, I always stood out as being different – stronger, unafraid, faster, taller, more able, and unwilling to accept the phrase *I am a girl* as an ending to any type of sentence that started with *I can't because.*

I have never been afraid of the dark, had any fears or suffered from any phobias that I can recall. Clowns, spiders, snakes, and bugs have never caused me to scream and run the other direction. Many times I've seen girls or women scream toward the closest available male *well, do something with it!* when they encountered a bug, spider or snake. I never had the luxury of being able to ask someone to *do something with* a bug or spider.

I'm sure I had one as a child and simply can't remember, but I have no actual recollection of ever having a nightmare or bad dream. My nights in bed have always been filled with somewhat peaceful thoughts of tomorrow, and what might be required of me to get through it without fault or failure. If for some reason I failed, I knew the only person I could blame was me. As a result, I was not only my worst critic, I was my only critic.

And critical of myself I became.

Now, as an adult, I am confident I am as strong of a woman as could ever exist. If it can be done, I can do it. If anyone is able to endure it, I am able to endure it. No other woman is more capable than I, this I know to be true.

I now lay in bed using every ounce of courage I possess to assist in my becoming stoic.

Until tomorrow.

Tonight, as the silence pressed into my chest like a heavy weight, I found it more difficult to continue to breathe. A lifetime of a blaring television I once viewed as an annoyance I would now welcome as if it were the softest music to my ears. The screams of *Victoria I need more pills, I'm in pain* which caused me to roll my eyes in agony as I searched the streets for a black market substitute, I now yearn to hear.

I realize my mother is gone, and although I accept it as being just what it is, I am finding it troublesome to live with the *change*. A lifetime of repetition doesn't necessarily make accepting change impossible, but without a doubt I have found it to be challenging.

My time away from Parker is time I have found increasingly difficult to live with. Being without him at my side is a simple reminder I have no desire to live my life alone. In some respects my mother's departure from this earth freed me, and now I yearn to be captured.

Snatched from my life of silence and kept safe from any further changes for a lifetime of lifetimes.

I feel if I expressed my desire to spend all of my available time with Parker *to Parker* it would cause him to view me as weak and incapable. As a result, I lie in silence and wait for something to startle me from my current state of desire.

Anything.

One moment of unwelcomed silence is more disheartening than a lifetime of incessant screaming.

And the silence deafens me.

PARKER

We'd spent the entire trip to the jeweler discussing the intricacies of a diamond. I had received quite a lesson from Kenton regarding the four C's of a diamond; cut, color, clarity, and carat weight. After his best effort to explain everything in detail, he insisted he do the all of speaking at the jewelers, to which I conceded. It was further agreed although he may do the negotiating, I'd certainly choose the diamond ring I personally preferred and felt I could afford.

Considering Kenton's chattering like a chipmunk for the extent of the drive, it was apparent he was far more excited about my proposing to Victoria than I ever would have expected. In the short walk from the parking garage to the jeweler, Kenton's pace was twice the speed of what Downes and I were walking.

"Christ, you two. Come on. We haven't got all damned day," he grinned as he all but skipped down the sidewalk.

As we rounded the corner and approached the entrance, Kenton burst through the doors as if he were walking into a saloon in an old western movie.

"I thought we'd go to *Robbins Brothers*. I don't know that I have any business in here," I gasped as we entered the *Harold Stevens Jewelry Studio*.

Kenton stopped walking and turned toward me, "*Robbins Brothers*? Does a true gentlemen take his wife to *McDonald's* for a meal to celebrate their anniversary?"

"No sir," I responded as I looked toward the display cases.

"That place is a chain store. Like *McDonald's* or *Taco Bell*. As you've assured me, this is a once in a lifetime event, so you're going to want a once in a lifetime diamond," Kenton shook his head in disbelief as we stood inside the doorway.

"Now let's have a look, shall we?" Kenton said as he motioned toward the well-lighted cases full of jewelry.

"Welcome to *Harold Stevens Jewelers*, My name is Ryan, how can I assist you gentlemen?" the man behind the counter asked as we approached.

"Ryan, I'm Kenton, to my right is Parker, and behind me, Downes. Parker is going to propose to the woman of his dreams directly, and we're in the market for an engagement ring. We need to see what you have. Round, colorless, clear, of the finest cut, and only if they exude sophistication from their every facet," Kenton chuckled.

"Well, congratulations, Parker. And it's a pleasure to meet you Kenton, Downes," Ryan nodded.

"Have you a carat size you're hoping to see? And regarding price range, where would you prefer to begin and end?" Ryan asked.

"We have no limits, Ryan. Our only concern for the time being is quality," Kenton responded proudly.

I turned toward Kenton and raised my eyebrows. Immediately I was met with a scowl and a pat on my shoulder by his right hand.

"Well, the new Celtic inspired rings by MAEVONA are quite breathtaking. Maeve Giles has a commitment to excellence as is apparent by her clean lines and distinct feminine style. My only fear is once you've seen one, nothing else will suffice," Ryan smiled.

"I fear nothing. And we'll require proof," Kenton chuckled as he squeezed my shoulder in his hand.

Ryan walked to the end of the case and removed a small display of twelve rings, a few of which were fitted with diamonds. They were all gorgeous in their own individual design, but one clearly stood out as exceptional. Close to the center of the display, in a combination of the brightest silver and gold metals, and fitted with a massive round diamond was the most breathtaking example of jewelry I have ever seen.

"Oh my," I stammered as I pointed to the ring in the center of the display.

"Breathtaking, isn't it?" Ryan half whispered.

"Quite," Kenton breathed.

Ryan pulled a cloth from his pocket and carefully removed the ring, "This particular piece is the iconic award winning Celtic solitaire diamond ring design *Eriskay*. It's by Maeve Giles, of course. This is the first edition. As you can see, no side stones, just your center stone. It needs nothing else. We can have one designed and fitted with a stone of your choosing."

"Weight?" Kenton asked as Ryan carefully handed me the ring.

I grasped the cloth in my fingers and held the ring between my thumb and forefinger. It was a true work of art.

"The stone as fitted is five point two two carats," Ryan responded.

"Well?" Kenton whispered.

I looked up and smiled, "I love it. It's…it's…perfect."

One corner of Kenton's mouth curled into a smile, "Perfect, huh?"

I nodded eagerly.

"Color?" Kenton asked as he looked down at the ring.

"Colorless."

"Clarity?" Kenton asked as he admired the ring.

"VVS1, the stone was hand-picked to compliment the ring's design, and intended to be used for our display of the MAEVONA line." Ryan responded.

I admired the ring, turning it in my fingers as I marveled at the light refracted through the stone. One could easily get lost in the beauty of the diamond alone. It isn't any wonder women are drawn to such beauty.

"Price?" Kenton breathed as he continued to admire the stone.

"It isn't our intent to sell this particular piece, Kenton. It's used to lure prospective customers to the MAEVONA line. It appears to be working rather well."

Kenton looked up from admiring the ring, "My boy Parker believes it to be *perfect* for his beautiful Victoria, Ryan. Everything can be bought. The price?"

"Three hundred thirty two," Ryan responded.

Thousand.

He means thousand.

Three hundred and thirty-two thousand dollars.

As my knees buckled, I almost dropped the ring. I felt as if I was a little boy again, and someone had just let all of the air out of my birthday balloons. I held the ring for a moment to save some embarrassment, and extended my arm toward Ryan and smiled.

"Give us a moment," Kenton whispered as Ryan accepted the ring.

His hand still resting on my shoulder, Kenton slowly turned away from the display and faced the entrance of the store. Slowly, he slid his hand across my upper back and rested his arm along my shoulders. Softly, he pulled me in closer to his chest, as if her were preparing to tell me a secret.

"Let me take care of this for you, son," he whispered.

"Kenton, no. Absolutely not. This isn't remotely close to proper," I hissed through my clenched teeth.

"How much money have you saved?" Kenton asked.

Although I had been proud of the amount of money I saved for the ring, I now looked down at my feet as I responded, somewhat embarrassed, "Ten thousand."

Kenton paused for a moment. I stood without speaking and stared at my feet as I continued to fill with shame.

"Would you give me thirty dollars? Right now? If I were getting married, that is?" Kenton whispered.

I looked up from the floor, "Absolutely."

"Well, thirty dollars is the same percentage to ten thousand that three hundred thousand is to one hundred million. I have far more than one hundred million, but let's consider only the money I have safely tucked away at four percent. Let's see..." he paused.

"I'll make three hundred and thirty thousand this month in interest alone, on my *money* that is. Look at it as a wedding gift Parker, the equivalent of a *thirty dollar* wedding gift. The more I think about it, I'm a cheap bastard," he raised his eyebrows and waited for my approval.

I looked down at the floor as I nervously swirled the toe of my right shoe in a circle, "Kenton, I can't allow you to buy the engagement ring."

"Fine, *you* buy it. But, I insist upon your acceptance of my wedding gift a little early. *Today,* that is. I'll have Downes write you a check for a million. It's the minimum I'd give in cash as a gift to the two of you," he pressed his index finger against the bottom of my chin until my gaze met his.

"Fine," I whispered, "*after* we're married. I can't accept it now."

Kenton shook his head slowly, "Alright, you little smart ass. Now, ask yourself this. On your wedding day, I'll hand you a fucking gym bag with a million dollars cash in it. Mark my words. I will. And as you hold that bag of money, smiling from ear to ear, would you have any regret of not being able to use a portion of it for this ring today? Something your wife will wear for a lifetime?"

I thought about his statement. I certainly would wish I had been able to spend a portion of the money today. This particular ring was gorgeous – there would never be another like it.

I nodded my head, "I would, yes. But this isn't proper. It isn't right. We should just leave."

Kenton comically raised one eyebrow, "You stubborn little fuck. Okay, look at it like this. I'm going to loan you three hundred fifty thousand today. Buy the ring. Propose. If she says yes, you'll have a nice wedding gift of a million cash on your wedding day. You can repay me at that time. Look at it as a simple loan. You're borrowing the money from me. If she says no, give me the ring back. The bottom line? *You* bought the ring with *your* money. Fair enough?"

It made perfect sense and saved me some embarrassment. Three hundred thousand dollars was an enormous amount of money to spend on a ring, but at this particular moment it seemed rather reasonable, considering all things.

I studied his face, "A loan?"

He nodded once.

I made an unsuccessful attempt to hide my excitement. As my mouth formed an embarrassing grin, I responded, "Fair enough."

Kenton's head immediately swiveled toward Ryan, "We'll take it," he shouted excitedly.

Ryan's face quickly changed to one of disbelief, "Sir?" he asked, still standing with the ring in one hand and the cloth in the other.

"The Celtic ring. The five carat display. We'll take it," Kenton turned to face the display case.

I cleared my throat as I turned to face Ryan. In two steps, I was standing at the edge of the case. I realized I shouldn't touch the glass, but I wanted to make a statement. Proper or not, I placed my hands against the leading edge of the glass, and looked him in the eye as he stood holding the ring. His face began to fill with confusion.

"*I'll* take it," I smiled proudly.

Ryan smiled and wiped the ring with the cloth he held, "Fabulous, Parker. We have many options in regard to structured payment. Let me get the paperwork."

As I was turning toward Kenton for verbal direction regarding the payment, he responded to Ryan.

"We'll pay cash. Or a wire transfer if that's acceptable," Kenton glanced toward Downes as he spoke.

Downes nodded his head once. Kenton turned and tilted his head toward Ryan, "Wire transfer?"

"A wire transfer would be acceptable, yes," Ryan grinned as he laid the cloth down and reached under the display case.

Ryan produced a business card and held it at arm's length, "Let me provide you with our account information."

Kenton reached for the card with his left hand, and without looking, fluidly flipped his hand over his shoulder as he held it between his thumb and forefinger. Downes took the card from Kenton's hand and smiled. Immediately, Downes turned away and removed his cell phone from his inner jacket pocket. It was as if they'd performed this maneuver a hundred times.

As I stood in front of the display and attempted to catch another glimpse of the ring while Ryan polished it with the cloth, Kenton stepped back to my side and placed his hand on my shoulder.

"Ten to fifteen minutes for the transfer," Downes said sharply from behind where we stood.

"Well, that should give me time to get the certification for the stone from the safe and quickly polish it for delivery, excuse me gentlemen," Ryan said as he turned and walked toward the rear of the store.

"Well, I'm sure Victoria will be quite shocked and rather pleased. So, what about the wedding? Soon?" Kenton asked.

"I'd prefer it to be, yes. You know how I am, rather conventional. Well no, I think they call it *old school* now. I feel a need to get her away from her mother's house and have her live with me. It's something I can't do in the absence of marriage. We can't live together out of wedlock, I wouldn't dream of it," I responded.

Kenton grinned and squeezed my shoulder in his hand, "One of the many things I like about you Parker, one of many."

As I silently stood and waited for Ryan to return, I realized although Kenton wasn't my *biological* father, he had taken on many of the duties of a father. Through the course of our friendship, even initially, his advice to me was always well thought out, and noteworthy. His excitement over my announcement to propose marriage to Victoria was quite cute, and far from what I had expected. All in all, I viewed Kenton as the closest thing to a father I could ever expect to have, and for this I was truly grateful. Filled with gratitude, I tilted my head toward him and smiled. Without speaking he smiled in return.

"Thank you," I breathed.

"For?" he asked in a whisper.

"For..." I hesitated.

"For being you."

PARKER

I stood at the window staring out into the courtyard as I held the ring tightly with the polishing cloth the jeweler so graciously provided. I turned the ring in my fingers, causing the light to reflect through the diamond differently. Each facet changed colors with the minutest movement of my hand. I had been standing here for no less than an hour admiring the ring and trying to develop a way to meet Victoria for dinner and *not* tell her I wanted to marry her.

As excited as I was, Kenton remained far more enthusiastic than I. For a man who found *zero value in telephone conversations*, he had called half a dozen times in the last three hours asking when we were going to have dinner next. His level of excitement was beginning to cause me to become more nervous, if that was even possible.

If you have something you feel a need to say, simply say it. Anything more causes you to look foolish and indecisive.

I often wonder if my grandmother will haunt me until the day I die. It seems everything I question in life, if she hasn't already provided the answer, Kenton surely will at some point. Considering the vast knowledge regarding life the two of them share, it's a shame they will never have an opportunity to meet. I walked to the table, wiped the ring free of smudges, and placed it in the velvet lined slot of the crystal box. Then, I picked up my phone and scrolled to Victoria's number, and pressed *send*.

Before the first ring was complete, she answered.

"Hey," she breathed into the phone.

"How do you feel?" I asked.

"Oh, pretty good now. I took some Tylenol and my headache's gone. Probably just too much time in the sun, I'm guessing."

"I see. Well, I'm glad you're feeling better. So, Kenton was wondering when we'd like to come over to eat. He's itching to get together," I asked.

"When?" she asked.

It sounded as if someone was juggling broken glass in the background. I held the phone at arm's length, and the noise remained audible.

"What are you doing?" I asked.

"Oh, sorry. Looking for bobby pins."

The noise stopped.

"When are you thinking?" she asked.

"It's up to you. Whenever you're up to it, I suppose."

The broken glass sound began again.

"Pick me up in an hour?" she asked.

I rotated my wrist and glanced at my watch. 4:30. Leaving her house at 5:30, we would arrive at Kenton's house by 6:00, which should work well for Kenton.

"Sure. 5:30?" I asked.

Over the sound of crushing glass, she responded, "Sounds great. I better get ready."

I shook my head as I wondered where she kept her bobby pins. "I'll see you in an hour."

"Paaaaarkeeeeer?" her voice trailed along as she said my name.

I smiled, "I love you."

"That's better. I love you, too."

"Goodbye, dear," I said.

"Ta-ta."

I hung up the phone and scrolled to Kenton's name and pressed send. The phone only began to ring, and he answered. Odd, considering he doesn't even carry a cell phone. I heard a faint breeze and seagulls in the background. He must have been sitting outside on the deck with it clutched in his hand.

"How does six o'clock sound?" I asked.

"Tonight?" he asked.

"Yes, if that's alright."

"Alright? It's *my* idea," he laughed.

"Well?"

"Sounds great. Now, we're not going to tell her tonight, right?"

"No, *we're* not."

"Downes, get Karen busy cooking something *special*, but not *that* special," his voice was muffled somewhat as he spoke.

His voice changed to a more serious tone, "Well, as much as I'd love to, I don't have time to talk all night on this damned phone, Parker. I've been sitting here staring out at my ocean for the last four hours. I have to prepare for tonight, get cleaned up and such. Have you anything else?"

"No sir," I chuckled, "I sure don't."

"Very well. I'll see you in a bit."

"See you then," I agreed.

The phone went silent.

As much as he tried, Kenton's attempts of late to maintain a professional posture were becoming unsuccessful. Hiding the fact that he was excited for Victoria and I proceeding with our life of love was far more than he was currently capable. I reserved hope he could make it through one night without blurting out some statement or comment which would let the cat out of the proverbial bag.

With my nerves shot and forty-five minutes to spare, I needed to find something to occupy my time besides staring at the ring. I looked around the room for something to entertain me. On the kitchen island sat the contract – in the same location it had been for a month. Not that it mattered so much *now*, but to kill what spare time I had and to provide a little entertainment, I stood and walked to the island. After picking up the stack of paperwork, I flipped through the pages and wondered where to begin. I certainly couldn't read it all in the amount of time I had.

Maybe I should start at the end and read it from back to front.

I flipped to the last page and worked my way forward without actually reading any content until something caught my eye.

The word *marriage*.

14 (d) Marriage: If, during the course of employment, the undersigned employee becomes married to a third party introduced through the course of his employ, the employer reserves the right to either terminate employment immediately or extend the contract indefinitely, at the sole discretion of the employer.

Post marriage contract extension will eliminate all necessary obligations on the part of the employed. Employer post marriage obligations will continue. Rate of pay to the employed during post marriage extension will increase at 20% (twenty percent) per annum.

I re-read the *marriage* portion again. Considering Kenton's promise of a healthy wedding gift, I was not necessarily worried about continuing employment or collecting wages, in fact, the entire thought of the contract not all but sickened me. Yet. This portion of the contract fascinated me. It appeared Kenton originally intended to either commit to pay me for life or terminate my employment based on *who* I was going to potentially become married to.

Interesting.

Two thoughts entered my mind.

What were the requirements to receive a lifetime of employment without obligation?

And.

Why?

VICTORIA

In Kenton's home, I have always felt safe. I have no way of attempting to determine exactly *why*, and I'm not convinced it really matters. In guessing, I'm sure a portion of it is having Downes present. After what little time I have shared with him one on one, I have no doubt he would give his life to save any of our lives, he just that type of person. With Kenton, I feel safe, loved, protected, and cherished. He's truly like the father I always wished for and never had.

And Parker.

In Parker's presence, nothing else matters. *Nothing.* I feel loved, cherished, and as if everything is complete in my life. With Parker, I feel as if I have stepped into the final chapter of my life – my journey to the ending – and I am not making the trip alone. I'm taking it with the one person I know I have the capacity to love for as long as I'm living.

In hindsight, I suspect having all three of the men in my life that love me in one home is what causes me to feel the way I'm feeling. Regardless, I feel like a queen in the presence of these men. And, for all of their manners and typical proper behavior, for some reason, tonight it is as if I'm in a room full of fools.

"I didn't even know you had a formal dining room," I said as we sat at the table.

Kenton laughed an almost phony laugh, "I'm sure there are places in this home I'm not even aware exist."

Downes began to laugh, "I'd have to agree, Mr. Ward."

And then Parker chimed in, "I know I've spent all but every moment here on the darned putting green. Or on the deck drinking tea."

"Peach tea," Kenton chuckled.

"Yes, peach tea," Parker slapped his knee with his hand.

"With floating fibers," Kenton slapped his knee and began to laugh deeply.

Maybe it's an inside joke.

Kenton covered his mouth as he began to cough, "Boy, I tell you. Here lately I've laughed more than I have in years. I'm going to choke to death if I keep you two around, this is ridiculous."

He picked up his glass of wine and took a sip. As he lowered the glass to the table, he stopped coughing and covered his mouth with the back of his hand, "But I must admit, I love the company. Second to none."

"Second to none," Downes agreed.

"What is the deal with you guys tonight? I feel like I'm eating with a bunch of Parrots," I glanced at Kenton and turned toward Downes, waiting for some means of response.

Parker turned my direction, "Parrots? We're not repeating each other. And we're not acting weird, we're just having fun, reminiscing about old times."

I looked across the table at Downes, "Before we ate, you three sat and repeated each and every word, phrase, and sentence the one before you made. When Downes began talking about Kenton's round of golf at Torrey Pines, it was ridiculous. I heard the word *outstanding* no less than a dozen times."

I shifted my gaze toward Parker, "Whatever. Fine. You three dorks keep playing your little game and doing whatever it is you're doing, but I'm on to you. And if a clown jumps through a doorway or some shit, I'm going to punch it. It's like waiting for a surprise birthday party you know is coming."

Kenton jumped from his chair, "Nothing's coming, nothing at all. Is it Downes? Parker? No surprises here."

"No sir, Mr. Ward. Nothing at all. No clowns, that's for sure," Downes responded.

Parker stood from his chair as soon as Kenton stood from his, "Nothing going on here. And certainly no plans for anything, not at all. Just a simple dinner."

I looked around the room and shook my head in disbelief and wonder. These three idiots were up to something, and it was apparent. I picked up my wine glass and drank the little remaining wine from the glass.

"Fine, let's go out on the deck," I said as I stood from my chair.

"Out on the deck it is," Kenton snapped.

"To the deck," Parker smiled and began walking around the corner of the table.

Downes stood without speaking as I rolled my eyes. I imagined stepping out onto the deck and balloons being tied to each of the chairs, a clown sitting against the handrail making animal shaped balloons at our request as we ate cake and ice cream, drinking root beer through the little curly crazy-straws.

"All I know is this – the next time I'm here, I want things to be back to normal," I said as I walked past Downes and into the door leading to the main hallway.

Kenton stopped walking and turned to look over his shoulder, "The next time? When shall we gather next? Parker?"

Standing between Kenton and I, Parker looked up, "Pardon?"

"Victoria wants to get together *again*. When shall we do it?" I'm free *tomorrow*," Kenton raised his eyebrows and glared at Parker.

I shook my head and attempted to walk past, "You're free *every day*."

"Point well taken, I am. Parker?" Kenton said as he reached out and wrapped his arm around my waist and pulled me into him.

"Let's do it again tomorrow. Same time, same dining room?" Parker asked as he placed his hand on my shoulder.

"Whatever, just be sure you three goons have all of this bullshit out of your system," I laughed.

Kenton hugged me and breathed, "I'm sorry, dear. I think we're all just excited about the sub-par round I shot on the south course at Torey Pines, a lifetime achievement which has been on my bucket list for some time now."

"That's fine. And I'm proud of you. Let's just make sure tomorrow's an entirely different story," I sighed.

Kenton took a short shallow breath and smiled, "Oh I'll make sure of that. Tomorrow will be an *entirely* different story, mark my words."

And for some reason, I truly believed him.

VICTORIA

Change is the difference from what it *is*, or what it would be if it were left alone. In life, oddly enough, the definition of change is not accurate at all. If we leave our lives alone, as they were, we continue to subject ourselves to all types of change. At any moment, life has the capacity to change, good or bad. To believe we have control over where and when these things happen is to believe we control the destiny of our lives.

My life has been a constant reminder that I am *not* in control, and I must live with the changes, like them or not, as they unfold. So far, I really don't have any complaints, but at times I sure have hoped I had a little warning to allow me to properly prepare.

"Wow, when I said I didn't want the same shit all over again, I didn't think I'd get *this*. Why all of the somber faces?" I asked as we sat at the table and waited for Karen to finish preparing the meal.

"Just hungry I suppose," Kenton responded.

Downes nodded.

And Parker attempted to find a comfortable spot in his chair, which for the first thirty minutes of the evening he didn't succeed doing. Something has been wrong lately, and I was not sure what it was. I realize I have no control over when and why things change, but accepting change isn't easy for me. Not always.

"I want the old crew back," I complained.

"Maybe after we eat," Kenton sighed.

Downes nodded.

And Parker continued to fidget in his chair.

I turned toward Parker, who was seated on my right side, "What the fuck is wrong with you? You've been squirrelly all night. Sit still."

Parker turned toward Kenton and complained, "I can't take it anymore."

Kenton stood from his chair and started to pace the length of the dining room.

"Can't take what? The wait? Surely it won't be much longer. Take off your jacket, you look flush. Are you okay?" I asked.

"No. I'm fine. I just..."

"What?" I asked.

"I am just. Yes, I'm hot. And I'm nervous. And I'm hungry. I haven't eaten since yesterday evening. I'm just," Parker stood from his chair.

"I'm sorry," he apologized.

He half knelt beside my chair and looked as if he were going to vomit.

"No need to apologize, dear. Stand up, you're making a fool of yourself, and if you barf on me, I'll going to be mad," I shook my head and reached for my glass of wine.

Parker cleared his throat, "Victoria."

Kenton stopped pacing the room and covered his mouth with his hands. I looked up at Parker, who was visibly shaking. His face was now covered in beads of sweat. I looked up at Kenton, who was audibly crying. He knew something I didn't.

This son-of-a-bitch is going to break up with me.

I fucking knew it.

I pressed my hands into the edge of the table and pushed my chair away enough to stand. As I stood, Parker stood along with me.

"If you've got something to say, say it Parker. *Say it,*" I demanded in a stern tone.

Parker tilted his head toward Kenton and then faced me again, "I...uhhm," he stammered

"For the love of God, Parker. Just do what you have to do. Get it over with," I shouted as I fought back tears.

Kenton's crying was becoming louder. I considered storming from the room, and quickly realized Parker was my ride home. *Great, this is going to be awkward as hell.* As my lip began to quiver, I bit into it, attempting to make it stop. Parker nervously reached into his jacket pocket, but didn't pull his hand out.

What the fuck is going on?

"Victoria, I'm sorry. I wanted to do this differently. It isn't working. So I'm just going to say it," he paused.

I fucking knew it.

"Victoria Lillian Fisker, I want to spend the rest of my life living," he pulled his hand from his blazer and held it curled up at his side.

Living what? Single?

You little prick.

He raised his hand in front of my chest and turned his fingers upward, "As your husband. Will you marry me?"

Holy. Shit.

"Oh my fucking God, Parker. Yes. Yes. Yes!" I screamed and dove into him, knocking him to the floor.

As we embraced into a long passionate kiss on the floor, Parker held his arm out to his side, still holding what I was assuming was the engagement ring. I had yet to actually *see* it, but I didn't care. I heard the words, and that's all that mattered. He could produce an aluminum foil ring, and I'd happily be his wife forever.

"Karen, hold the meal," Kenton sobbed loudly.

The tone of his voice raised into what became a broken shout, "Bring…champagne."

As our lips parted, I arched my back to look into the face of the one man I truly ever loved. As I did, he moved his hand between us and held the ring in front of me. Immediately, a lump developed in my throat, and I felt as if I were going to be sick. I attempted to swallow twice. My throat felt as if it were filled with sand.

"Place it on her finger, son." Kenton coughed.

I spread the fingers of my shaking hand and watched as Parker slid a ring onto my finger that every woman on this earth would soon envy almost as much as they envied my fiancé.

I looked down at the ring, "Its…"

"It's…perfect."

"Well…get up…off the…floor," Kenton said between sobs.

We both stood from the floor at the same time, covered with smiles from ear to ear. There is probably not much on this earth that can be said to truly drive a girl to a point of immediately going numb. The type of numb she'll feel once in a lifetime, and never feel again. I now know, having been through what I just went through, what has the ability to make every nerve in your body go useless.

Four simple words.

Will. You. Marry. Me.

"Let me see it," Kenton said as he stretched his arm over the table.

I held my hand over the table proudly and raised it to meet Kenton's. Downes stepped into the light of the chandelier and shaded his eyes as if he were being blinded. As Kenton's hand met mine and raised it slightly, I felt as if he were my father, approving my engagement to my lover.

"I'm so happy for both of you. For us all, actually," he said as he wiped tears from his face with is free hand.

"I'd also have to say, Victoria, that has to be a first," he chuckled.

"What's that?" I asked, still feeling like I was in shock.

"Oh my *fucking* God, Parker. Yes. Yes. Yes," Kenton whispered.

"I did *not*," I gasped.

Kenton nodded.

I looked up at Downes.

He nodded.

And at Parker.

He nodded.

"Oh, honey. I'm so sorry," I pushed my lower lip out for sympathy.

"I wouldn't have expected anything less," Parker laughed as he wiped the sweat from his brow.

"Nor would I," Kenton sighed.

"Nor I," Downes agreed.

As we all sat down, Karen carried in a tray with champagne glasses and a bottle of champagne, "Here you are, Mr. Ward."

Kenton quietly nodded his head toward the table.

"Thank you, Karen," Kenton said as she placed the tray onto the edge of the table.

Kenton began to pour champagne into one of the glasses, "So have you given any thought to *when*?"

I turned to face Parker, who shrugged his shoulders, "I don't see much value in waiting or having a long engagement, do you?"

I shook my head excitedly.

"Well, if I may," Kenton said as he handed a glass of champagne to Parker and me.

As soon as we accepted the glasses, he continued, "I'm of the opinion most have a lengthy engagement because they're partially not certain, and or to assemble the family for the wedding. This, for the most part *is* the family," he motioned around the room.

And he was right. This *was* our family, our only family.

"As soon as possible, if I have much of a say. I'm quite ready to begin living together," Parker sighed.

I thought of my sleepless nights at home alone, and the difficulty I have had being away from Parker since my mother's death. I didn't want Parker to feel rushed, or as if I was incapable of waiting.

But considering what he said…

"I'd wait just short of forever, Parker. You *know* that. I'm comfortable with what we have, or I'd be happy to marry you tomorrow. I really would. But you're right, there's no value in waiting. I'm ready," I smiled.

Parker looked up toward Kenton and smiled as he lifted his glass of champagne, "Soon," he grinned a she nodded his head.

Kenton nodded his head and raised his glass, "Here's to *soon*."

And we all raised our glasses and toasted.

To being married.

Soon.

VICTORIA

For as long as I have lived, I would say I've only had two wishes. More like dreams, I suppose.

As a toddler and a young girl, I often wished I had a father. My mother's constant complaints of his death and her love for him continued to remind me how much she missed having him in her life as well. As I grew older, I began to understand the differences between all of the other girls in school and myself. They had families, and I did not. They sat at home at night at a dinner table and ate with their brothers, sisters, and both of their parents. I sat at home and ate Ravioli's from a can as my mother sat in her chair and watched television in what I assumed was terrible pain.

Life as a little girl in my home was far different than most other girls I knew. I never felt that a father was a fix, but I felt it would be a good start. Not only could he take care of my mother, but he could also take care of me, I was sure of it. He could cook me meals, and tell me stories, and hold me when I was scared. When there were things in school I did not understand, and there were plenty, he could softly explain in a manner I could understand. He would always love me, and never let me go.

He would drop me off at school and pick me up when it was over so I didn't have to walk alone. When the other children's parents came to school for their conferences, he would come. And teachers would not stand in the hallways and talk about him in a tone that I was perfectly capable of hearing.

But a father never came.

As I grew older, and hormones began to run rampant inside of my preteen body, I yearned for a boyfriend. One who would hold me, love me, care for me, and never leave me. When I turned thirteen, my wish was granted. Josh Wilson asked me to be his girlfriend. Although it was through a note passed in class, I took it for being the gospel. We went steady for about a month, all of which was a one-sided relationship from an emotional standpoint. He played sports, ran around with his male friends, and never cared to spend time with me outside of school.

At my insistence, he agreed to spend an evening with me at my home. My mother agreed, and I was sure this was going to take our *relationship* to the next level. How wrong could I have been? Half an hour into the night, he demanded I have sex with him, and when I said no, he called me a slut and stomped out. Later, while back in school, there were times I wished I would have had sex with him. He did what I believed to be unthinkable – he told the other boys he *did* have sex with me. It wasn't long and all of the boys were begging me for sex and calling me a slut when I said no.

And I slowly began to lose trust in all men.

What began as my second wish turned to more of a dream – to one day become married to a man who would accept me for who I was and what I believed. I knew regardless of whom it was I may ever meet, sex was going to wait until we were married. That, to me, was an absolute.

I wished and dreamed throughout high school, and every boy, upon finding out I was a virgin, decided they were not interested. I stopped with the daily dreaming, and came to understand marriage may *never* happen for me. By the time I was twenty-one years old, and had not yet had a boyfriend, I completely gave up on being married; and on men in general. My attitude quickly changed, and for the most part, I became anti-social. My lack of interest in meeting men turned into a lack of interest in meeting people.

And life, to me, became quite simple.

Two wishes and two impossibilities.

And low and behold, I was introduced to Parker Bale and Kenton Ward. Now, as a girl of twenty-three, I have one of my wishes granted. I am soon to be married, and I have a man who I *view* as a fatherly figure. He may not be my father, but he's as good as I could ever hope for.

And far better than most biological fathers, I'm sure.

I just needed one thing from him, if possible.

As I nervously approached the gate, a voice came from the landscaping along the fence.

"Good afternoon, Miss," the voice hesitated.

"Good afternoon, Victoria. Mr. Ward is expecting you."

"Downes?" I asked.

"Yours truly. Come in and park by the fountain."

As the gate opened, I depressed the clutch and revved the engine. Although I never wanted Parker to see my car, I had no problem with Kenton seeing it. I just needed to make this a quick visit. Parker had gone to get fitted for a tuxedo, and he would be done in about an hour. I released the clutch, mashed the gas, and lurched forward along the driveway that led to the Ward Mansion. As I came to a stop at the fountain, the engine died.

Perfect timing.

As I stepped from the car, Downes walked out onto the porch, "Good afternoon dear. I hope all is well."

"Very well, thank you," I said as I slammed the door to the car.

"Vintage Toyota, they're bulletproof," Downes nodded his head and smiled.

"Oh stop it. Good God, Downes, it's a piece of shit," I laughed as I walked toward the steps.

"Kenton's sitting out on the deck. Follow me," Downes said as I reached the top step.

I followed Downes through the house and out onto the deck. As I stepped through the French doors, Kenton stood from his seat, smiled, and opened his arms, "This engagement isn't going to last forever, and surely you're going to go the distance, aren't you?"

I laughed as we embraced, "Yes, I'm going the distance, it's not that."

"Money? Do you need money?" he whispered as he hugged me.

"No, it's not that. I really just wanted to talk," I said as I released my grip and stepped back.

"Okay. I'm all ears, dear," he said as he sat down and picked up the pitcher of tea.

"Peach?" I asked.

"I've completely forbidden that damned raspberry, yes it's peach," he smiled.

I nodded my head.

As he poured a glass of tea, I considered how to begin what it is I wanted to say. This wasn't going to be easy, and I hated the thought of rejection, but if I didn't ask, I certainly would never happen. If I did ask, it just might. For a once in a lifetime event like my marriage, I had to at least ask.

"Do you love me?" I asked as he was still pouring the tea.

He stopped pouring and lowered the pitcher to the table, "Yes, I do. With all of my heart."

"Good because I love you too. You *and* Downes. And I'm not including him because I think that's what you or Parker wants, I am because it's true. And Kenton, you've become the closest thing to a father I could ever have hoped for. I consider you so much more than a fatherly figure. So much more," I said as I reached for the tea.

"What's troubling you, Victoria?" he asked softly.

I had no idea how to do this. I guess it's just best to do it.

"Would you consider," I paused for a moment and took a sip of tea.

"Let me rephrase that. I would like for you to stand up for me in my wedding. Would you do that? You know, give me away? Please?"

His lip began to quiver as he attempted to open his mouth. Slowly, and without much stability, he quietly stood and turned toward the ocean. As he grasped the handrail of the deck, he began to speak.

"Victoria, I'd…" he raised his clenched hand to his mouth and cleared his throat.

"I'm sorry. Yes, I'd be. I'd be honored," he said as he continued to look out at the ocean.

Here comes the hard part.

I stood and walked around the table to the edge of the deck. Without facing him, I walked to his side and gripped the handrail beside him. As I stood near him, I became relaxed. Kenton's presence allowed me to feel content; and as a feeling of comfort washed over me, the scent of the beach filled my nostrils.

And at that moment, I knew.

"Would you…"

This is not going to be easy to ask.

"When they ask. However it is they ask, you know. When they ask," I paused and attempted to gather my thoughts.

My voice filled with emotion, I attempted to continue, "When he asks *who gives this woman?* Would you stand with me? You know, stand with me and say…"

Filled with hope, I continued to stare out at the ocean, "*Her father.* Would you say that for me? I've always wondered when this day came what I'd do, and I just…I really want you to walk down the aisle with me and say that. When they ask. *Her father.*"

I tilted my head to the side to face him.

Tears ran from his eyes and dripped from his chin. His knuckles turned white as he gripped the handrail and took a few deep breaths. And I waited. Smoothly and slowly he inhaled a breath through his nose and turned to face me. He lifted his right hand from the handrail and held it to his mouth as he coughed a few times to cleared his throat. And he responded with the words I had hoped for.

"I'd be honored, my dear."

And just like that. Both of my wishes were granted.

DOWNES

The thought of spending a lifetime loving a person who in turn loves you unconditionally is something I have yearned for a lifetime to obtain. To have witnessed Parker and Victoria develop or naturally possess a love such as this satisfies me to no ending. Love is something impossible to explain. It is said, and I must agree, love must be experienced. My having played a part in what is before me will remain with me for a lifetime.

Parker stood arrow straight in his black tuxedo as the music began to play. My arms neatly crossed in front of me, I stood and waited for the sound of the door opening. As the door creaked, I tilted my head and glanced over my right shoulder.

The beautiful dress Kenton insisted on purchasing flowed behind her as she walked down the aisle. Her arm wrapped in Kenton's, they walked slowly down the flower covered floor. Kenton had spent tremendous time and effort to ensure this wedding was something that everyone in attendance would enjoy and remember. He believes the mind has a more vibrant sense of recollection if a scent is associated with the respective memory. Well over a five thousand flowers were used to line the floor of the entrance with pedals. The beautiful aroma thickened the air and made breathing a sheer thing of joy.

As they stopped at the end of the aisle, the preacher took a deep breath and clutched his bible tightly in his hands. Over the top of his glasses, he studied Victoria and Kenton and smiled.

"Who gives this woman to be married to this man on this beautiful day?" he asked.

"I do. Her father," Kenton responded sharply, his voice echoing throughout the church.

He had practiced those four words for the last two weeks, over and over. On several evenings, he had me ask the question repeatedly. More than anything, he wanted to be able to respond without a tremendous amount of emotion in his voice. Above all, he wanted the wedding service to be remembered as one of perfection.

The preacher smiled and lowered the bible from his chest to above his waist, "I've never met a father who was completely willing to give up his daughter, so may I also ask, do I have your blessing for this marriage?"

Victoria tilted her head toward Kenton and waited.

Kenton arched his back and cleared his throat slightly, "Yes sir, you certainly do."

Victoria turned to face the preacher and her soon to be husband. The preacher motioned for her to step to up onto the platform beside Parker. As her dress trailed behind her and Kenton stood proudly, Victoria stepped gracefully up the two steps and stood beside Parker.

The preacher smiled and raised the bible to his chest. He glanced at Parker and turned toward Victoria, "We are gathered here today, on this happy and joyous occasion, to join this man and this woman in holy matrimony. The book of Ecclesiastes reminds us *two are better than one, because they have a good return for their labor. If either of them falls down, one can help the other up. But pity anyone who falls and has no one to help them up. Also, if two lie down together, they will keep warm. But how can one keep warm alone? Though one may be overpowered, two can defend themselves. A cord of three strands is not quickly broken.*"

He paused and lowered the bible to his waist, "Marriage is a solemn institution to be held in honor by all, it is the cornerstone of the family and of the community. It requires of those who undertake it a complete and unreserved giving of one's self. It is not to be entered into lightly, as marriage is a sincere and mutual commitment to love one another."

"This commitment symbolizes the intimate sharing of two lives and still enhances the individuality of each of you," he hesitated and nodded his head in the direction of both Parker and Victoria.

Again, he raised the bible to his chest, "And from Matthew, book nineteen. *Haven't you read the Scriptures? They record that from the beginning God made them male and female. This explains why a man leaves his father and mother and is joined to his wife, and the two are united into one. Since they are no longer two but one, let no one split apart what God has joined together.*"

"Will rings be exchanged as a symbol of this union?" the preacher asked.

Parker nodded his head sharply.

The preacher smiled, "A ring is a fitting symbol for a wedding promise. It is a circle with no beginning and no end. Love without end is what we hope to achieve in marriage. As this ring is placed upon your fingers remember that it is your love for one another that has brought you here, and it is that love that will guide you down the pathways of your future. You may place the ring on her finger."

Parker removed the ring from his pocket, and without instruction, repeated what he had practiced, "With this ring, I give you my heart. From this day forward, you shall not walk alone. May my heart be your shelter, may my arms be your home."

And he placed the ring on her finger.

The preacher turned to Victoria and nodded, "You may place the ring on his finger."

Gracefully, she reached for the ring Kenton had sewn on the side of her dress with a fine thread. As she snapped the thread, she raised the ring, and repeated the verse she and Kenton had spent many evenings practicing.

"I give you this ring as a symbol of our marriage. For today and tomorrow, and all of the days to come."

And she placed the ring on Parker's finger.

He turned to face Parker and smiled, "Parker Landon Bale, do you take this woman to be your wedded wife? Do you promise to love her, comfort her, honor and keep her in sickness and in health, remaining faithful to her as long as you both shall live?"

Parker nodded his head sharply, "I certainly do."

Kenton's light weeping beside me reminded me of his presence. I lifted my arm and placed it on his shoulder. The preacher slowly turned to face Victoria.

"Victoria Lillian Fisker, do you take this man to be your wedded husband? Do you promise to love him, comfort him, honor and keep him in sickness and in health, remaining faithful to him as long as you both shall live?"

Victoria turned to face Kenton and hesitated for a split second. As I held his shoulder in my hand, he shuddered and nodded his head. Victoria turned to face the preacher.

"Yes sir. I do," she responded.

"Then," he alternated glances between the couple.

"Then by the power invested in me, I now pronounce you husband and wife. You may kiss the bride."

And they embraced, for the first time, as husband and wife.

PARKER

Once you're married, things begin to change. I have heard variations of this phrase said many times. Generally, when repeated, it is intended to advise the recipient that marriage ruins things, or makes relationships worse. Nothing, to me, could be further from the truth.

Victoria and I, now married for two weeks, could not be happier. To imagine anything to change from the beautiful days we now have would be difficult. I have no reason to believe that if we both love one another, and we certainly do, this could or would ever change.

We had already decided to sell her mother's home, reside in my condominium, and look for another home in which to permanently reside. Kenton held true to his promise of the wedding gift, but in lieu of cash, transferred money into my bank account. He would not, however, take payment for the ring, insisting if I attempted to pay him, he would merely deposit an additional three hundred thousand into my account. Mention was made of the contract language regarding *gifts purchased*, and that the cost was to be borne by the employer, to which we both got a good laugh.

Last week, at dinner with Kenton and Downes, we announced our intent to have a child or children, and to do so naturally, by the grace of God. One never knows, but without birth control, maybe the near future will bring a child into our lives. Nothing would make Victoria or me happier.

Today, as Victoria continues to add her touch of decorative flair to the condominium, I'm off to the mansion to have a talk with Downes.

Although I am not one hundred percent certain, I believe Kenton's birthday may be approaching, and a surprise party is in the works.

The gate opened as I pulled into the drive. As I approached the home, it was if it was for the first time. I seemed to be viewing the estate with different eyes than I had previously. The trees were taller, the estate larger, and grass greener, the home more grand. Taller. More magnificent. In approaching the fountain, I noticed luggage on the porch beside the top step and the front door was propped open. Downes stepped onto the porch as I stopped the car.

"What's going on?" I asked from the bottom step.

"Mr. Ward has been called to Chile to meet with an investor. It was somewhat of an emergency meeting, but what will more than likely be very rewarding. He's already flown out. He asked that I tell you some things. As the meetings will be in the mountains, he will not have cell phone service, but he will be able to communicate via email daily. He asked that you communicate in that fashion," he paused as he adjusted the bags on the porch.

"What's with the luggage?" I asked, motioning toward the luggage which littered the porch.

"I'm heading out now. I'll be assisting him in the negotiations. Hopefully it'll only be a few weeks. The Chilean's are a difficult bunch to deal with, or I guess I should say *previous negotiations have gone poorly*."

"So, you'll *both* be gone for two weeks?" I asked.

It felt strange to even say. I had spent time with Kenton and Downes on an almost daily basis for the last six months, and to not see either of them for two weeks would seem odd. In some respects I suspect it could be a welcomed change, allowing Victoria and I some time alone without feeling a need to rush out and do something. At any rate, the thought of not hearing Kenton's voice was somewhat unsettling.

Downes bent his knees and lowered himself to the top step and sat down, "Yes, regretfully so. Mr. Ward asked that you pry a few of those dollar bills from your account and take the wife on a small vacation."

I rolled my eyes and sat down on the bottom step, "Maybe so. I suppose we have no reason not to now. We'll need to kill some time with you two away."

"Do you need a ride to the airport?" I looked up and asked.

"No, I'll leave the car in the extended parking," he responded.

"Please, let me take you. There's no need…"

Downes interrupted before I finished speaking, "No, I'll drive myself. I have no idea of when I'll return."

"Very well," I lowered my head and stared down at the stone drive.

"Please, take some time for you and Victoria while we're away. Kenton insisted," he placed his hand on my shoulder and squeezed lightly.

"I didn't even see you come down," I grinned as I looked up.

I thought about what he said. Victoria and I could kill some time while they were away, and possibly have fun somewhere nice. We had yet to take a honeymoon, and had spent all of our time moving her into my condo.

"Maybe so. We'll see. I'll let her know when I get home that you're gone and see what she says. So you need any help?" I asked.

As he knelt beside me, his hand still resting on my shoulder, he responded, "No. Go be with your bride. I'll load the bags. Just…"

As I stood from the step, he opened his arms and hugged me, "Just take care of her, Parker."

Parker, he called me Parker.

"Now and always," I smiled.

As my car rounded the fountain and headed for the gate, I felt empty and somewhat scared. As I waited for the gate to open, allowing me to exit, I looked in the rearview mirror. The estate looked back at me in the form of a reflection.

And it appeared extremely small.

PARKER

Victoria and I had been on the road for almost three weeks. Although we had received an occasional email from either Downes or Kenton, it was almost as if it really didn't matter – at least not now. Our time spent on vacation had been filled with events and sights which consumed us. Neither of us had previously spent much time outside of California. Personally, my feet had only been planted in two states, Ohio and California. Victoria's in California alone.

Until now.

After a drive along the Pacific Coastal Highway and through northern California, we ventured to Las Vegas. After a week of sightseeing and shopping we were exhausted of the lights, noise, repeated buzzing, bells, and screaming from the gamblers. A short drive from Las Vegas, and we arrived at the Grand Canyon; where we found comfort, relaxation, and a sense of well-being neither of us had ever known.

"We've been here for a week," Victoria grinned from her perch above the south rim of the canyon, standing on a large stone.

"I could stay for another," I sighed.

"It's just…"

She turned to face me, "It's just so breathtaking – every part of it. And like I told you the other day, it makes everything else in life seem so insignificant and small."

"I agree. Some people ask for proof of God's existence. One look at this," I motioned out over the canyon, "and they'll need nothing else."

"Precisely," Victoria agreed.

Her blonde hair blew in the light breeze as she stood and stared into the canyon. Today, for whatever reason, her eyes seemed a little greener and much less brown. Although her appearance was always one of beauty, she seemed much more beautiful today – standing in the sun – than she ever had previously. Slowly, I walked toward her as she absorbed the magic the canyon offered. As I reached to brush her hair behind her ear and expose her face, she tilted her head to the side, allowing it to fall.

I wrapped my hand softly around the base of her neck and leaned into her, kissing her deeply. As we continued to kiss, as with every time in the past, I filled with a sense of contentment – a sense of knowing. Knowing Victoria and I would remain together until, as Kenton had previously stated, the bitter end.

As our lips parted, she grinned, "I love kissing you, Parker."

"I love," I hesitated, released her neck, and smiled, "you."

She smiled and stepped down from the stone which she was standing on and scanned the horizon. As she placed her hands on her hips, she inhaled a deep breath, closed her eyes, and exhaled. As she opened her eyes, her lips parted slightly and took another shallow breath.

"I want to come back. Often," she said as she gazed toward the canyon.

I nodded my head as I stared into the canyon, "I agree."

"It's easy to become just a little more spiritually in tune with things here. It's," she paused and raised her hand to her mouth.

"Therapeutic," she smiled.

While she continued to stare out into the canyon, I felt my phone buzzing in my pocket. Surprised and somewhat apprehensive, I removed my phone and cleared the screen. To my pleasure, I had received a text message from Downes. Grateful to have received a text and not another email, I grinned. This would mean they were in the United States or at least close to it. Anxiously, I opened the message.

Parker,

I need you to come to the mansion immediately. Please, at least for now, I request you keep this to yourself and come alone.

Downes

I blinked my eyes and stared at the screen, attempting to develop an understanding of what might be going on. I glanced toward Victoria, who was kneeling and drawing with a stick in the sand, unaware of my having received the message. Carefully, I slid the phone into my pocket and began to walk her direction.

"There's been a break in at the mansion. Downes has asked that I check for what may be missing. We need to go," I fibbed.

She dropped her stick into the sand and stood, "Did he call the police?"

"Kenton doesn't like involving the police unless absolutely necessary. They've asked that I check for them. They're on the way home," I said nervously.

She raised her hand to her mouth, "It could be dangerous."

"Not now. Whoever it was will be long gone. It'll take us ten hours to get home. No worries, baby. Just a quick home inspection," I held my hand to my side.

As she gripped her hand in mine, we turned and began walking toward the car. As I opened the car door for Victoria and watched her get in, I attempted to convince myself I wasn't *lying* to her. Ultimately, I was *protecting* her. Protecting her from whatever it was Downes didn't want her to see.

And I didn't want to know.

PARKER

Our ability to accept life's difficult offerings is a testament of our relationship with God.

"What's wrong?" I asked as I ran up the steps.

Downes was dressed in exercise pants and a tee shirt. He stood, his face grave, and held the door open. As he raised his head and attempted to speak, I realized he looked much different. It was as if he hadn't slept or eaten in days.

"He..." Downes paused.

"He wants you, Parker." He swallowed heavily and patted me on the shoulder.

"Where is he? Tell me what's going on. Is he okay?" I walked through the door nervously, and in no way prepared for a response.

"He's at the end of the hall, in the guest bedroom," Downes responded.

"Follow me," he said.

As I walked into the room and looked up, I immediately wished I hadn't.

Kenton lie in bed in the center of the room, an I.V. attached to his arm, and a good thirty pounds lighter than when I saw him last. Beside where he lay, a chair sat facing the bed with the stand which held the bag attached to the I.V. beside it. As my mind realized it was in fact Kenton, I groaned.

"Kenton," I fell to my knees on the floor beside the bed.

Slowly, he opened his eyes, "Sit, son. I have..."

His eyes closed and breathing sounded very labored and wet. As he attempted to speak again, he began to cough deeply.

"So much to…tell you," he coughed.

I turned to face Downes. Quietly, he nodded his head, turned, and closed the door behind himself as he exited the room. Reluctantly, I faced Kenton again. As I did, I began to blurt out questions, hoping for answers which would support a quick recovery.

"What happened? Did you ingest something in Chile? Are you going to be okay?" I wiped my nose with the back of my hand.

Before Kenton was able to respond, the bedroom door opened. Downes walked in holding a rather large syringe and quickly made his way to the opposite edge of the bed. As he knelt beside Kenton and pulled the blanket away, exposing Kenton's frail arm, I raised my eyebrows in wonder.

"It'll allow him to talk to you for a while without much difficulty or pain," he responded.

"Morphine?" I asked.

"Not exactly," Downes shook his head.

"It acts like a steroid – a very *strong* steroid. This should give him an hour before he passes out again. Please, pay attention," he stood and walked out of the room, closing the door behind him.

Again, I turned to face Kenton. This entire event seemed so surreal. Just a matter of weeks ago, Kenton was fine, or at least he seemed like it. I covered my face with my hands and began to quietly cry.

And pray.

"I need to come clean, son," Kenton's voice was deep and rumbled from his lungs.

"What happened?" I asked as I wiped my face.

Slowly, Kenton raised his hand and extended his index finger, "Shhh. Let me talk. I have so much to say."

I nodded.

"Parker, I haven't been totally truthful," he said slowly.

I shrugged, not knowing what to say.

"I learned of you years ago," he said as he pointed to a glass of water sitting on a night stand beside the bed.

I reached for the water glass and sat in the chair beside the bed. As I handed Kenton the cup, I realized he was incapable of holding it. His hand was unable to grasp the cup and hold it firmly. I tilted the cup to his lips and poured a small amount of water into his mouth. As he blinked his eyes, I removed the cup and held it in my shaking hand.

"Learned of me?" I asked, confused.

Again, he held his finger in the air.

"I haven't got much time," he breathed, "let me talk."

I nodded.

"Tallert. He was a professor at your college. He's Downes father," he took a shallow breath.

"He told us of you one night about two years ago. When your grandmother died," he raised his hands and wiped his lips.

I knew I recognized that name from somewhere.

He explained how you were a phenomenon, an anomaly…he said you were a four point zero student in high school, and the same in college. He explained of your gentlemanly behavior. And he explained although," he took another shallow breath.

"Although he didn't learn from you directly, he learned from another professor, one you were friends with, that you were a virgin. He spoke of your moral values, and the fact that he wished all modern men were a little more like you."

"Zenner?" I asked, "Professor Zenner?"

Kenton nodded.

Professor Zenner and I had become close during my time at college. I had confided in him on many occasions after my grandmother passed, and an equal amount before. He seemed quite impressed with my grades, and my ability to understand everything which was taught to me. I was fascinated with his family history, and their involvement in World War II. I stayed many a day after school and shared thoughts with him.

"I did a background study on you and found out about your parents. Your grandfather and your grandmother. And I waited…" he paused.

"For you to graduate. You see, son. I *needed* you."

I shook my head in wonder.

He raised his finger again and lightly shook his head.

"The story I told you. The woman in the restaurant. Downes and I. In 2005?" he raised his eyebrows slightly.

I nodded my head, recalling the story of the woman with a daughter and no husband. The spiritual awakening which caused Kenton to become the fine man he is today.

"It wasn't exactly true. That's when," he paused and began to cry.

He raised his hand to his face and attempted to wipe the tears from his eyes. As I reached for his face, he shook his head, "I need…this."

"That's when I found out I had a daughter. One I never knew of. After obtaining a strand of her hair through a Private Investigator, I confirmed what I had been told. She was my daughter. One I had never known existed," he tilted his head to the side.

"I can find her. Downes and I can find her," I sat up in my seat.

"I can bring her here. Where is she?' I asked frantically.

"It's…" he paused and raised his hand, pointing toward the south wall.

"It's Victoria."

PARKER

In light shock, and rather confused, I stood from my seat.

"Sit," Kenton said as he pointed to the chair.

"But. I don't..."

He raised his index finger, motioning for me to listen.

"Twenty-three years ago, I met her mother in a bar. She was one of many. A bar fly, and what I later learned was a virgin the night I met her. I never knew," he shook his head and began to cry again.

"We had a one-night stand. And Victoria is the result. I didn't know until I found out through a friend of a friend who had prescribed her mother's painkillers. There aren't many doctors who make house visits these days, and he was one of them. He had diagnosed her chronic pain from a fall at work, and was describing the condition of her hip to me. Although she was young," he paused and pointed to the cup of water.

After a sip of water, he continued, "her bone disintegrated. He was fascinated. He was further fascinated by the fourteen year old girl who brought him a plate of food she'd prepared while he was there."

He hesitated and shook his head lightly, "The girl? Victoria. When he mentioned the mother's name, I sat up in my chair, recognizing it from years before. *Fisker.* An odd name," he nodded.

"After a little investigation, and a bit of her hair from school, I found out," he closed his eyes and remained still.

I had so many questions. My mind began to race. None of these things explained his health. Or his current condition. Or anything. Confused, I stood and began to pace the room.

"What's wrong with you? No bullshit."

"I found out about seven months ago I had lung cancer," he began to cough deeply.

"I opted for no treatment, and to die. I figured it's what I deserved. But, before I left his earth, I wanted to introduce you to Victoria, and hope for the best."

"That's when I started placing advertisements to try to lure you to me," he nodded.

"They didn't work," he began to laugh and the laughing brought a coughing spasm.

"We knew from the Private Investigator she spent all of her time away from home at the bookstore. Downes developed the idea of the ad which finally got your attention," he shook his head slightly, as if embarrassed.

And it all began to make sense.

"That's why the contract stated I had to go to the bookstore?" I asked as I stared at the wall above him.

He nodded his head.

"Seven years," he breathed.

I shook my head in wonder.

"I waited seven years to actually meet her," he paused.

"And for someone like you to come along," he smiled.

"Why didn't you tell her? Earlier? Why don't you tell her now?" I asked.

He shook his head, "I couldn't let her find out. And I can't. Her mother told her the father died immediately after her birth. And she stuck to that story. Her mother was all she ever had. To tell her otherwise would ruin her trust of her mother, and in turn, their relationship."

"All for a little self-satisfaction and selfishness on my part?" he closed his eyes.

He opened his eyes and began to cry. As he contained himself, and the crying slowed, he opened his eyes and looked my direction.

"And the greatest three gifts God could ever give me," he hesitated and raised his hand.

"Meeting her," he raised one finger.

"Meeting you," he raised another.

"And giving my little girl away at her wedding," he raised the third finger.

I attempted to digest everything he had said, and began to break down. As I started to cry, I covered my face with the palms of my hands and began to blubber. This was too much to understand, comprehend, and accept.

As I fought to regain my composure, Kenton spoke.

"When you decided to propose, I began to second guess my decision to die from the cancer. Everything was going so well, I decided maybe I did deserve to live. I decided after the wedding I'd go to a specialty hospital and seek emergency treatment."

"You weren't in Chile?" I asked, feeling stupid after I did so.

He shook his head.

"I was in Texas. At a specialty hospital. MD Anderson. The best. They tried, but, it was too late. Now? It's running through me like a river," he sighed.

"How long do you have?" I asked.

"About ten minutes for the medicine to wear off. And maybe a day from what the doctor said," he shook his head and closed his eyes.

"I'm sorry, son." he whispered.

I suppose many people would be angry, feel lied to and maybe cheated. I, on the other hand, did not. I know Victoria and I were meant to be together, regardless of the circumstances which brought us together. I wouldn't trade the fact that we were married for anything on or of this earth. Kenton, to me, had been and continued to be nothing less than the father I never had. He was a gentleman, and a very intelligent man regarding living life and doing so in a manner which would cause others stand and take notice.

"I have two requests," Kenton whispered.

As I attempted to speak, my voice faltered. I nodded my head.

"Never tell her who I am. Don't ruin her mother's name."

I nodded sharply.

"Promise me, Parker," he sighed.

I nodded my head and cleared my throat, "You have my word."

"And. Bring her here. To see me. Before I die."

I nodded again.

I turned toward the door, not really knowing what to say. My throat had developed a lump making it difficult to breathe, let alone speak.

"Parker," Kenton grumbled.

I turned to face him.

"I love you, son."

I turned to the door, and grasped the knob in my hand. I squeezed the knob tightly and turned it slow. As the door opened, I faced the open hallway and spoke.

"I love you too," I hesitated, staring out into the hallway.

Slowly, I turned to face Kenton, and continued.

"Father."

PARKER

"Parker explained everything on the way here. I'm here. I love you so much." Victoria was well composed, considering all things.

Kneeling beside the bed, she held his hand in hers while Downes and I stood and watched. Downes explained why he wasn't able to give Kenton another shot for a few hours, and how it might cause heart stress or a heart attack. Kenton's breathing was noisy and labored, as if his lungs were full of water. The shot Downes gave earlier had clearly worn off, leaving him no means of medicinal assistance. As Kenton opened his tired eyes and smiled, Victoria leaned into him and kissed his forehead.

"You know," she paused and looked toward Downes and me.

Kenton raised his hand and wiggled his fingers. I walked to the opposite side of the bed and lowered my hand to meet his. Slowly, his fingers wrapped around mine as he gripped my hand lightly in his. I found it difficult to see Kenton this way, and made a conscious effort not to look into his eyes. As I stared across the bed at Victoria, she smiled and continued speaking.

"You're not just a friend to me. You haven't been since that night out on the deck when I asked you to stand up for me as my father. On that night it kind of *began*, I don't know. It's tough to explain," she paused again and looked into Kenton's eyes.

Kenton half-smiled and blinked his watering eyes. As Victoria began to speak again, he closed his eyes. It was as if her words provided him a certain comfort – an escape from the pain.

"But to me, the day of the wedding it all changed. It all came together," she began to cry lightly.

"Now. *Right now?* Kenton Ward," She paused again and wiped her tears.

"You're my father. I want you to know that," she leaned over him and kissed his forehead again.

As Kenton squeezed our hands simultaneously, his eyes still closed, he fought to develop a smile on his face.

In a dull whisper, he responded, "And you're my daughter."

Kenton coughed twice, slowly opened his eyes and whispered, "Until the bitter end."

The grip on my hand slowly loosened.

His eyes closed one last time.

And he passed away.

PARKER

The time which followed Kenton's death was nothing short of a blur. The arrival of the ambulance, removal of the body from the home, all of the discussions…everything would become hazy when I attempted to think of it.

So, I've chosen not to think of it. Since Kenton's death, neither Victoria nor I have returned to the mansion. Downes has kept somewhat to himself after the death, which is what I would have expected. His relationship with Kenton was very unique. They had developed a bond over the years that couldn't be questioned.

The funeral service arrived before I was mentally ready, but I don't know that we ever actually become truly prepared. As I sat in the funeral home, looking at a casket I knew was empty, I reserved a little hope that this was all a joke; and Kenton would run into the room, waving his putter and laughing. Regretfully, this never happened.

Considering Kenton's life of solitude, I was pleasantly surprised to see roughly one hundred people at the service. With Downes seated at my side, I looked up toward the lectern where Victoria stood. Her strength and devotion caused me to swell with pride.

In the black dress she had carefully chosen, and her blonde hair in a bun, she looked magnificent. Kenton would be proud of her insistence to provide the eulogy. It seemed as she'd been standing there for some time, but in actuality, it had only been a matter of seconds. As I blinked my eyes and looked around the room, she cleared her throat and began to speak.

"Kenton Ward was a man amongst men. He was an unselfish man, and gave far more than he ever took. One day at his home, after the passing of my mother, I stood on the back deck and stared out at the ocean, hoping for some sort of answer as to why she had passed away."

"As I stared out into the water, a whiff of the beach filled my nostrils. I've always looked at natural aromas such as the beach as being a gift from God – his proof to us of his existence. When we attempt to inhale them eagerly, as I often do, they disappear. Well, on this particular day, at least initially, the scent came naturally. As I always seem to do, I inhaled sharply and lost the smell."

"I stood and continued to stare at the ocean, aggravated for some time, hoping for it to return. It wouldn't. Angry, I lashed out at my now husband and Kenton, mentally blaming them for my having lost the smell. Standing there with my nostrils filled with the smell of the beach, I had developed a manner of accepting my mother's death; and I wanted to the scent to return. A confirmation from God, if you will, that everything was going to be okay."

"Shortly, Kenton must have sensed something was wrong. He could do that, you know. He was a wise man with so much advice and such an ability to provide comfort. He stood to give me a hug, attempting to comfort me. As he held me in his arms, I became filled with a different emotion – one of love and acceptance. You see, Kenton accepted me for all that I am; my strengths and weaknesses, my shortcomings, even my foul mouth. He didn't care. He loved me none the less."

"As he held me in his arms, he told me he loved me, and I settled down. In having that conformation of his love, nothing else really mattered. He continued to hold me for an amount of time I can't even come close to describing. Rocking back and forth on his heels, it was as if he were rocking a baby to sleep. And naturally, the scent returned. In my mind, it was God telling me everything would be alright."

"I've never had a father. Well, I *had* a father, but he died immediately following my birth. So, from birth to present, I have not had a father in my life. Not until I met Kenton. Recently, after my boyfriend proposed to me, and we were beginning to plan the wedding, I went to Kenton's home. Kenton and I were standing on the back deck, facing the ocean. It was a common place for us to talk. I had some things I needed to ask him, and I was trying to develop the courage to do so. Prior to asking him, once again, I naturally smelled the beach, and the scent all but immediately vanished. Nervously, I asked if he'd consider giving me away at the wedding. He graciously accepted. It didn't really surprise me, considering Kenton was Kenton. He was a giver. I had one more question to ask," she hesitated as he voice stammered and wiped the tears from her cheek.

"When a man and a woman get married, and the preacher asks *who gives this woman to be married?*" she paused and wiped her eyes again.

"I wanted to know if Kenton would respond *her father*. I wanted him to give that to me. To not only give me away, but for one day, my wedding day, to actually *become* my father."she paused, bent at the waist, and raised both hands to her face.

After a momentary pause, she stood and lowered her hands to her side, "When I asked him if he'd stand beside me and respond, *her father*, as if he were my father...I gripped the handrail of the deck, stared out at the ocean, and waited. At the same moment that he responded, the scent of the beach returned. I knew at that moment, *I knew* – everything was going to be alright. He said *yes* by the way. You see, Kenton Ward gave me what I have yearned to have for my entire life. Kenton Ward became *my father*. A father I never had," she paused and wiped her eyes again.

She sniffed lightly and continued, "Kenton will be missed. By all, I am certain. But for me? For me? Every time the scent of the beach fills my nostrils, and it happens naturally, as if God provided it...I'll know Kenton has returned," she paused and wiped the tears with the back of her hand.

As her hands cleared her face, she concluded, "just to stop in and tell his daughter he loves her."

As I wiped the tears from my eyes, I glanced around the room and watched as everyone else did the same.

After the service, as we were leaving, I saw a familiar face. Standing by the door stood Hec Astur. I hadn't seen him since the first day I met Kenton. His green eyes glistened as he smiled and extended his hand.

"Downes, Parker, and you must be *Victoria*," he said as he gently shook all of our hands.

As he shook Victoria's hand he smiled, "Hec Astur, pleasure to finally meet you."

As he released her hand, he nodded his head toward Victoria, "Kenton will be missed for sure. Touching eulogy, I must say. Brought tears to my eyes."

Hec smiled, "Crying is God's way of cleansing our souls."

"So, thank you. I needed it," he nodded his head once toward Victoria.

"Parker, I need you to stop in and see me. Tomorrow if possible," he raised his eyebrows and waited for a response.

"Alright. I'll do that," I responded.

"You remember where?" he asked.

I nodded.

Hec turned to Victoria and lifted his chin slightly, "Again. Victoria, thank you, it was so very touching. As sure as I'm standing here, Kenton's looking down you now, proud as a peacock."

He smiled, and turned away.

"Who was that?" Victoria asked.

"A friend of the family," Downes quickly responded.

As we turned toward the door, Downes winked. It was nice seeing him slowly return to normal. I'm sure it would take some time for all of us to return to a routine state. Kenton was a powerful man. As we walked toward the B7, Downes turned toward Victoria and me.

"Peach tea on the deck?" Downes asked.

"I thought you'd never ask," Victoria responded.

PARKER

Sitting in the same seat I sat in waiting for our first meeting, I sat and waited to see Hec. I smiled at the thought of one of Kenton's first questions to me. I waited almost a week to come to the office, but considering all things and the recent changes in my life, I felt it was the soonest I could break away.

"Are you a risk taker, Mr. Bale?"

I wouldn't consider myself a risk taker, but on that particular day I became one. I took a risk, and the reward will remain with me for a lifetime. Kenton may be gone from this earth, but his memories will fill my heart and my mind for all of eternity. Or, in the words of Kenton Ward, *until the bitter end*. The sound of shoes began to echo throughout the hallway. I looked up and to my left as the sound became sharper.

Lisa.

I stood and smiled.

"Mr. Bale," she extended her hand.

I lightly accepted her hand, "Lisa. Pleasure to see you again."

"I'm so sorry for your loss, Mr. Bale. I truly am," she whispered.

"Thank you. He will be missed for sure," I responded as I released her hand.

"Mr. Astur is waiting. Follow me?" she asked as she turned away.

"Certainly,' I responed.

As we walked past the door of the conference room, I peered in. The table where we first met sat empty. I paused, staring at the table, and smiled. For a fleeting moment, I stood and stared. As I heard Lisa's footsteps continue, the sound of Kenton's voice filled my mind.

"Drinking water from a bottle is akin to eating beans from a can, cereal from a box, peanut butter from a jar, or drinking wine from a bottle. A beverage is contained in a bottle for shipping and storage. It should remain in the bottle until it is poured into a glass, at which time it could be enjoyed. Do you drink your wine from a bottle, Mr. Bale?"

I stared into the room and mouthed the words.

"No sir."

"Mr. Bale?" Lisa's voice brought me out of the trancelike state I was in.

I turned to face her. At the end of the hall, she stood in front of a large wooden door.

"You'll be meeting in *this* room. Mr. Astur's office," she smiled.

Slowly, I walked to her side and stopped. As she opened the door, Mr. Astur stood from behind his desk and smiled, "Parker. Please, come in."

"Lisa, close the door behind you if you will," he said as he motioned toward the door.

"Nice seeing you, Mr. Bale," Lisa nodded.

"Likewise," I responded as I walked into the office.

"I'll make this brief, Parker. Well, as brief as possible. Would you like a drink?" he asked as he walked around the corner of his desk.

"Yes. Water," I paused and smiled, "In a glass please."

Hec smiled and shook my hand, "Please sit down, Parker."

I sat in a chair positioned in front of Hec's desk. The office was very large and obviously in the corner of the building. Both walls were constructed of glass, and looked out over the city of San Diego. A large desk sat at one side of the office, and behind it wooden cabinetry – which I assumed contained legal documents or books. On the other side of the room, a massive library of books, and a glass display case filled with various treasures.

As he walked past, he handed me a glass of water and a coaster. I took a sip of the water and placed the glass on the table beside me and crossed my legs. As Hec walked back to behind his desk, I smiled and waited patiently to see why this meeting was called. He crossed his legs as he sat and placed his elbows on the desk. His face somewhat sullen, he lowered his chin into his hand, and looked down at the desk.

"I have no way of knowing, so I must ask, Parker," he looked up from the desk and hesitated.

"Did Kenton explain to you the reasoning behind his seeking to employ you?"

I nodded my head slowly, "Yes sir."

His chin still resting in his hands, he nodded his head.

"Did he further explain his *relationship* with Victoria?" he asked.

"Yes sir, he did," I responded.

"Well, the fact he did will allow this to come a little easier for me, I suppose. It goes without saying, I'm sorry for your loss. I feel it as well, and I will for some time. Kenton was a great man and a damned fine friend. A difficult man for most to get to know, but for those he chose to let into his life," he paused and smiled.

"We're truly blessed, aren't we?"

I nodded my head, "Yes sir, we are."

"Now, down to the brass tacks, Parker. You don't mind my addressing you as Parker, do you? I should have asked," his eyes widened slightly.

"Parker is fine, yes sir."

"Very well," he tilted his head to the side and rolled his eyes.

"You know, that damned Downes says that all the time. *Very well*. And he got Kenton to saying it, and now I say it all the damned time," he smiled and stood from the chair.

He walked toward the window on the right side of his desk and looked out over the city. His cautionary proceeding with the meeting was making me somewhat nervous. I attempted to think of other surprises or hidden facts which Kenton may have forgotten, but couldn't conjure up any sensible scenarios. As my mind drifted from the room we were sitting in, Hec's voice brought me back to reality.

"You entered Kenton's life, and from what he shared with me, you changed him into a better man. One evening here, before he modified his will, he told me what pleasure he received from your visits. He went on to say he tried his best to provide you with advice, and guide you in living life, but that you needed so *little*. He found tremendous value in getting to know you, Parker," he turned from facing the window and pushed his hands into his pockets.

"Another evening, several months ago, he told me of a morning you two shared at his home. He was practicing putting, if I remember correctly. He told me he viewed you as a son he never had. He had become quite fond of you. He admired you, Parker," he pulled his right hand from his pocket and pointed my direction as he spoke.

"As you might have expected, Mr. Ward left a will. A very detailed will. And on that night, he changed it. Parker, life for you is going to change significantly," he paused and looked toward the display case.

"Everything, and I do mean *everything*. He left everything to *you*. There are conditions, Parker. But the estate, the wealth, the cars, all of the belongings, his investments, his company, *everything*. It's all yours," he began to walk toward the case.

I went numb. He continued to speak, but not a word was legible. In a matter of seconds, as Hec placed an ornate wooden box on his desk I began to regain my composure.

"This box contains Kenton's remains. You're aware he was cremated?" he asked.

I nodded and attempted to swallow.

"*One*. You scatter his remains in the ocean behind the estate."

"*Two*. You must *keep* the estate. It's yours, but only if you *keep* it. You may eventually choose to reside in another residence, or choose to move to another state, but the estate is only to be occupied by you and your family – and will always be your *home*," he paused and rubbed his chin in his hand.

"*Three*. Downes Tallert. Downes will remain in your employ. It's written into the will, you have no choice. He didn't want to separate what Kenton described as his *family*. Mr. Ward placed a large sum of money into a separate account and the interest from said account will be transferred into Downes' bank account as payment for his services. So, in short, you and your family – which includes Downes – will be the only residents of the home."

"And *four*. He asked that the family visit his grave on Memorial Day each year."

I sat and stared, still in complete shock. Slowly, I stood and walked to the window and looked out over the city. Off in the distance, toward La Jolla, I could see the same beach and ocean we often viewed from the deck at Kenton's home.

My home.

Our home.

Out of the corner of my eye, I watched as Hec walked to where I stood. As he placed his hand on my shoulder, he spoke, "Take a few days or a week to digest everything, Parker. Come in and see me. I'll do all I can to make this as easy for you as I am able. And, I must advise you, Kenton left me a sizeable sum to ensure I took care of your financial and legal needs. Anything you need, anything at all regarding the estate or investments, I'm here, *gratis*, at your service."

"Very well," I said, still staring out over the city.

As I spoke, I realized I too had developed some of Kenton's speech patterns. Something else he had left me as a reminder of our time together. Still staring over the city, my focus on the ocean, I began to speak.

"There is *one* thing I'll need you to do rather promptly. For my peace of mind," I said.

Hec squeezed my shoulder in his hand, "Name it."

I took a shallow breath, "I'll need you to advise me on setting up a trust, and a college fund."

"Easy work for me. May I ask…"

Before he finished speaking, I proudly responded.

"For the baby. Our child. Victoria's pregnant."

"Oh my word. Well, congratulations, Parker. Keep me apprised of the developments. And a trust will be nothing to set up. We'll have fun doing so. The pregnancy…that's sure exciting. It certainly didn't take you two very long," he patted my shoulder lightly as he chuckled.

After careful consideration of his statement and some serious thought, I responded, "You should live every day as if you're going to die at midnight. And ask yourself throughout the course of each day, *if this were my last day on this earth, would I do anything different?"*

"Wise words," Hec nodded his head and grinned.

"May I ask its origination?" he asked.

I turned to face the window and focused on the ocean once again as I responded.

"Certainly. He was my father."

EPILOGUE

Although I had very few problems with the baby to speak of, for some reason today was much different. After feeding, he had not burped. Now, he continued to cry and fuss. Parker's futile attempts to burp him were followed by Downes' who was also unsuccessful. Frustrated and tired, I wished there was something more I could do.

"I'll call the doctor if he continues," Downes sighed.

"We'll see. Maybe it'll naturally work its way out," I shrugged.

"Should we go ahead and try to go?" Parker asked

I nodded my head as I walked along the hallway, bouncing with each step.

"I'll pull the B7 around," Downes said as he walked from the room.

It had been about a year since Kenton's death. We had each found our own way of dealing with his death as well as his absence from the home. Having the home as ours was one of the best things for us all, and had certainly drawn us closer as a family. Karen stayed, which was a blessing in itself. Together, we had developed our own friendship, sharing recipes and taking turns cooking for the men. Her peach tea was something we all continued to enjoy during our time together on the deck – a reminder of things since passed.

Parker followed as I walked out onto the porch. The month of May in San Diego is about like every other month, and today was no exception – eighty degrees and sunny. Downes opened the door of the car as I approached, and I lowered the baby into the car seat. After buckling him in, I walked to the other side and got into the car beside him.

"Sit in front, Parker. I'll ride back here alone and relax," I sighed.

As Parker got into the front seat, I exhaled. For now, the baby was lightly fussing and attempting to fall asleep. It was a great improvement from earlier, as the morning had been filled with his constant wailing. I closed my eyes as the car began to maneuver through the long drive and away from our home. I knew the drive to the cemetery shouldn't take long. We'd all been there before, but this was our first of what would surely become many traditional visits. It was our first Memorial Day. Exhausted from the sleepless night, I fell asleep to the sound of the car's tires humming on the surface of the road.

"Wake up, we're here," Parker said as he opened the car door.

I blinked my eyes and focused on the gravestones along the horizon. I'd never been to a cemetery before my mother or Kenton passed away; my father had been buried in another state, and my mother and I never took the time to travel to his grave. I turned toward the baby who was sleeping.

"Want to take turns?" I asked as I motioned toward the car seat.

Parker shrugged, "I guess it'd probably be best. I love you. We won't be long."

"Leave the flowers, or at least some of them," I said out the open door.

Parker nodded his head and raised his index finger to his lips. I looked down at the baby as he quietly slept and smiled. I turned toward the door again and slowly pulled it closed.

"You shhhh," I smiled as I pulled against the door handle.

Parker and Downes weren't gone for long, and they returned. After Parker took my position in the back seat, Downes and I quietly walked to the gravesite. As we stepped to the gravestone and stopped, Downes handed me some the fresh flowers we had brought with us. Standing in front of the grave, clutching the flowers in my hand, I slowly lowered myself in front of the etched stone.

"Well, it's Memorial Day. Not that we need a special day to come visit, but this is the first of our family tradition. I'm sure Parker told you, but in case he didn't, I will."

"We have a baby. He was born six weeks premature, but he's doing really well. For some reason, today he's really fussy. Although I always do, I really wish you were here *today* to help. I know you'd find a way to fix it. And I didn't sleep much last night, so I need a hug. One like we had that day out on the deck. Remember? The one where you rocked on your heels?"

I paused as my eyes welled with tears.

"Oh, and there's a little more. We named him Kenton Ward. Kenton Ward Bale. We all call him *K.W.* because it's hard to think of having another Kenton in the house, at least for now. I love you. And I miss you so much. I'll be back soon. Maybe by then K.W. will be feeling better."

I stood from my crouched position and dropped the flowers beside the grave.

Goodbye father.

Downes wrapped his arm around me as I turned away. Together, we walked silently to the car. Downes didn't speak much, and he didn't need to. His facial expressions and his actions made his thoughts clear and left nothing to the imagination. What little he did speak was truly meaningful. I remain extremely grateful to have him in my life.

The drive home was uneventful and rather relaxing. Soft music kept the baby asleep, and we refrained from speaking to allow him to sleep. For the entire drive, I prayed when he woke up he felt better, and wasn't in such pain. As we pulled around the fountain, and came to a stop, I unbuckled the baby from the seat. Immediately, I realized my prayers weren't quite answered. He began crying and squealing as soon as I removed him from the seat's restraints.

"I'll take him for a walk," I said as I pulled him from the car.

I walked through the house and out onto the deck. Frustrated, I began to pat his back as I held him against my bosom and against my shoulder. He continued to scream and his stomach felt tight and bloated.

I continued to bounce in place and lean over the handrail as I patted the baby on the back.

Please God, help me. He's in pain.

As I prayed there be nothing seriously wrong with our baby, I patted his back lightly and bounced on my toes. I stared out at the ocean toward the location where we had spread Kenton's remains and attempted to find some inner peace. The day was clear, and minimal smog allowed me to see to the horizon. The water was the most beautiful of deep blue colors. As I absorbed the beauty of the ocean and hugged the baby, I remembered the day of Kenton's hug, and the smell of the beach. I closed my eyes and became lost in the memory as I continued to pat the baby.

The scent of the beach filled my nostrils. My heart raced. It lingered for the longest of moments, and continued as I took two conscious breaths. The baby burped and rested his head on my shoulder.

The scent of the beach still lingering strong, I opened my eyes and spoke out loud.

"I love you too, father. I love you too."

Made in the USA
Lexington, KY
11 January 2015